LO

"Wow, Annie," Barb whispered, as a tall young man in an Irish-knit sweater got up from the front row and walked toward the podium. "He's gorgeous."

She was right. Padraic McKinnon was absolutely the most handsome guy I'd ever seen in person. Thick black hair fell across his forehead. And even from where I was sitting, I could see his eyes were the most intense blue under his thick black eyebrows. His face was really tan—he looked like he'd spent the summer hanging out on the beach. But he looked sad, too. Sad and sensitive. I sighed. Where had he been all my life?

"Hi." He was addressing a crowd, but his voice was low and quiet, as though he were talking to just one person—a person he cared about. "Thank you all for coming to my poetry reading. Anyone here ever met a poet before?"

The room was silent.

He smiled. "I'm sure you have without even knowing it. We're all poets, you know, in some sense." He paused.

I realized I was holding my breath. My hands were gripping the edge of my chair, and my heart was pounding wildly.

BANTAM SWEET DREAMS ROMANCES

Love Lines

Frances Hurley Grimes

BANTAM BOOKS

TORONTO • NEW YORK • LONDON • SYDNEY • AUCKLAND

RL 6, IL age 11 and up

LOVE LINES
A Bantam Book / March 1990

Love Lines

Chapter One

"I don't care *what* Mr. Manson says," I told my best friend Barb as I followed her down the hall, which was crowded with kids rushing to leave school. "He can't *make* me go to this workshop. Who cares about dumb poets? Besides, I've been planning all week to go to the mall and have my nails done. Pierre's is giving free demonstrations—one every hour. If we hurry, we might even get picked."

"You're impossible!" Barb pushed back her long brown hair. "Your mother will kill you if you put those plastic things on your nails. Remember what happened when you wanted to bleach your hair?"

"Not bleach, highlight. And the nails aren't plastic. They're acrylic. I want red ones—bright red. I'm going to completely change my looks. I've decided I need to look more . . . interesting."

"C'mon, Annie, how many times do I have to tell you?" She frowned at me behind her glasses. "You look fine the way you are. I wish I had your wavy blond hair and blue eyes." She stopped

1

in front of the closed double doors that led to the school library.

"It's *frizzy,* dirty blond hair," I told her.

I sighed. What was the use of trying to make her understand? She was way too serious for only sixteen. Barb studied every night, and she even had a little basket on her desk where she kept brochures from colleges. Colleges! Imagine! I wasn't even used to high school yet.

Inside the library, it looked like most of the kids from Mr. Manson's English classes were already there. I followed Barb past the tables of talking kids until she finally sat down at an empty table in the back and immediately opened her history book.

So much for conversation.

"Sometimes you really embarrass me," I told her.

She looked up, confused.

"You're not supposed to study *all* the time."

Barb smiled and went back to her book on the American Revolution.

Bored, I looked around. Above the crowded bookshelves, the walls of the library were lined with pictures of famous writers. Old writers. They grimaced down at the tables through ugly glasses and bushy eyebrows. I nudged Barb. "Look at that picture of Shakespeare. Does he look happy? He's fat, bald, and ugly. And he looks bored. Like all the other writers in our English lit book."

Barb rolled her eyes and went on with her history.

I spread my hands on the table in front of me, examining the Pink Plum nail polish I'd put on the night before and the tiny pearl ring my parents had given me for my sixteenth birthday that summer. The ring was beautiful, but I didn't think it was exactly my style. I really wanted rubies or diamonds—something brilliant and exciting. But that was my life, I thought. I was a flashing ruby in a quiet, cultured-pearl family.

"Hey, you guys," Tommy Fitzgerald said as he put his books down on our table. He pushed back a strand of rust-colored hair and grinned at me. "Been practicing your jump shot?"

It was a standing joke between us. Tommy, Barb, and I had lived on the same block all our lives. We'd been friends ever since we'd played together in Tommy's sandbox. Even though Tommy had always been the tallest kid in our class, in eighth grade I'd challenged him to a game of one-on-one basketball. Of course he won. Right after that game I decided I liked everything about him, except the fact that he was better than me at basketball.

I crossed my legs and leaned back. "I'm still practicing. Some day I'll wipe you out."

Tommy laughed and slid into the chair next to me.

Some kids started clapping, and I saw Mr. Manson step up to the podium. He frowned in that way that made him look like a stern British schoolmaster, and everyone was quiet right away. "The attendance sheet is going around," he said, "and I'm glad you could all make it."

"Sure," Tommy whispered under his breath. "Make it or get an F."

"Most of you," Mr. Manson went on, "have

3

never been to a poetry reading, so this is a special first-time experience."

A few kids groaned.

"Padraic McKinnon," he said, pointing to someone in the front row, "is our honored guest today. He is a highly respected poet, despite his young age of only twenty-four."

"Young?" Tommy whispered. "Twenty-four's pretty old, if you ask me."

"He's been published extensively in *Poetry Digest* and has won several awards," Mr. Manson continued. "His latest award was the prestigious Lowell Prize for poetry."

I slouched down in my seat, straightening my sweatshirt. Dad had brought it back for me from his last convention. It was bright yellow, with an orange sun that had "Palm Springs" written under it. Pretty neat, I thought, for a girl who'd never even been outside of Massachusetts. I tugged at the sleeves and listened to Mr. Manson say, "I want you all to welcome Padraic McKinnon."

Some kids clapped, and a tall man in an Irish-knit sweater got up from the front row and walked toward the podium. From the back of the room, he looked kind of cute. I leaned forward to see better. He certainly didn't look like any poet I'd ever seen before.

"Wow," Barb whispered when he turned around. "He's gorgeous."

I nodded. She was right. Padraic McKinnon was absolutely the most handsome guy I'd ever seen in person. Thick black hair fell across his forehead. And even from where I was sitting, I could see his eyes were the most intense blue under his thick black eyebrows. His face was really tan—he looked like he'd spent the summer hanging out on the beach. But he looked sad, too. Sad and sensitive. I sighed. Where had he been all my life?

"Hi." His voice was low and quiet, as though he were talking to just one person—a person he cared about. "Thank you all for coming. Anyone here ever met a poet before?"

The room was silent.

He smiled. "I'm sure you have without even knowing it. We're all poets, you know, in some sense." He paused.

I realized I was holding my breath. My hands were gripping the edge of my chair, and my heart was pounding wildly.

"A poet sees the souls of things. He looks beneath the surface. In the face of a young girl, he sees past the outer person and into the depths of her being. Her fears. Her loves. Her very reason for existence."

I shifted uncomfortably in my seat. How could he see all that?

"People live their lives by pretending—to others and to themselves. Pretending happiness . . . love. We all need to look into our souls, to seek our own truths. I write to and from that place."

Do I have that place? I wondered.

He put his hand to his face. "My first poem," he said softly.

> Now there is nothing of you
> but the print of your lips
> on the rim of the wineglass
> A blurred remembrance.

> A pale pink smudge on the
> translucent crystal.
> I hold the fragile stem in my
> trembling fingers
> and bring the cold thin glass
> to my mouth.
> And taste.

"He's weird," Tommy said under his breath. "I mean, who ever thought about writing poems about lipstick smudges?"

"Shhh." I poked him in the arm but still sat on the edge of my seat, leaning forward. What happened? I wanted to ask. What did she look like, this girl with the lipstick? Why did she leave?

"He's so fantastic." Barb sighed.

I nodded, still staring. "But sad. Why is he so serious and sad?"

"Poets are always sad," Barb whispered back. "It's part of the job."

"This next one," Padraic went on, "I wrote"—he paused—"I wrote once when I was in love." He cleared his throat and began to read.

> Oh celebrate
> the wild, brilliant dandelion
> fertility unbound.
> Bright flash . . .

"This guy's crazy," Tommy whispered in my ear. "My dad hates dandelions. Gets a special weed killer to get rid of them. Want to get a pizza after this?"

I kicked him under the table, then folded my

arms and concentrated on Padraic for the rest of the poetry reading.

"And now," Padraic said almost in a whisper, when he had read several more poems, "I would like each of you to write a poem. Explore *your* feelings. I'll be conducting a poetry workshop after school on Fridays, and you're all welcome to come and read your poetry." He held up a sheet of paper. "I have a sign-up sheet here for anyone who's interested."

Mr. Manson thanked him, and kids started leaving, most looking relieved it was over. About ten girls clustered around the podium. Before I could even think about it, I joined them.

Mr. Manson raised his eyebrows when he saw me.

Up close Padraic was even cuter. He was handsome in a classic kind of way, like the stars in the old black-and-white movies—all square chins and straight eyebrows.

As each girl signed the sheet and moved away, I was able to get a little closer.

"Ah, Miss Thornton," Mr. Manson said. "I've finally discovered what you like to write besides notes to your friends." He smiled, his eyes crinkling behind silver-rimmed glasses.

I blushed. "I write poetry all the time," I lied.

Padraic handed me the sign-up sheet. His hands were tan, and his fingers were long and graceful.

"Ann Margaret Thornton," he said, reading my name after I'd signed it with a trembling hand. "You have a good name for a poet."

"Really?" My voice squeaked with pleasure.

"Absolutely. What do you write about?" His

eyes were gorgeous—a deep, deep blue. And they were looking right at me.

"I write about—about love," I told the eyes.

He seemed to study my face. What did he see? I wondered. Did he believe I could know about love?

"Love," I went on, flustered. "Love . . . is—is everywhere I look, too. In—in glasses, like you said, and—and dandelions. My last poem was about . . ." I looked around, frantic. ". . . about a love in a—a . . ."

Padraic's head was tilted a little; he really seemed interested.

Barb kicked my leg from behind.

". . . love in a shoe," I finished, ignoring her giggles.

Padraic raised his eyebrows. His eyelashes were thick and curly. "Hmm. A love poem about a shoe? I'd like to read it. Will you bring it to our meeting?"

I nodded, backing away.

"Come on!" Barb grabbed my arm and pulled me toward the door. "Let's go to the mall."

I looked at her, then back at Padraic, who was leaving by the side door. "Barb," I said, slowly and quietly, only half realizing what I was saying, "I don't care if I ever go to the mall again."

Chapter Two

George Washington once slept in my house. Sometimes on foggy nights I can almost picture him in his military uniform, sitting on the front porch and nodding his approval at the way Mom has fixed up the old place to look exactly like it must have looked when he stayed here—all polished wood floors, stenciled walls, and braided rugs.

"Why does everything in our house have to be so old?" I'd asked Mom when she redecorated my room last summer.

"There's beauty in tradition," she explained. "A sense of meaning, of timelessness . . ."

"I'd like my room to be all black and chrome. You know, with a black plastic futon and little chrome-and-glass tables? Barb's whole house is like that."

Mom just shook her head. "We've had this discussion before, Annie. I don't care what Barb's house looks like, and you cannot have a black plastic futon." She looked back at the paper. "Hey, here's an estate sale over in Westwood.

An old trunk would look great at the foot of your bed."

Fixing up our house is how Mom got good at doing what she does—interior decorating. When everyone in town saw what a terrific job Mom had done on our house, they all wanted her to do the same for their houses.

We're all really proud of her, but right now I was glad Mom wasn't home. I needed to make plans. And a quiet, empty house was the perfect place to do it. Up until today, my life's plan had been to become a cheerleader, own a red Porsche, and live in a mansion on the beach. But now . . .

"What do poets eat?" I asked Van Gosh, our cat, as he followed me down the hall to our kitchen. I turned on the radio for inspiration, and one of my favorite songs came blasting out.

I danced around the kitchen table, imagining Padraic was there, too. *You are so full of life,* he would say. *Such an inspiration. . . .* I would smile into his eyes and, between steps, pause and whisper something poetic back like, *Alas, my love . . .* I sashayed around the counter, throwing my arms up toward the copper pots that hung from a rack on the ceiling.

My darling, you dance divinely. . . .

I swirled around to find my older sister staring at me.

"Hi, Annie," Holly greeted me. Her blond hair was tied up in a knot, and she had on jeans and a faded purple sweatshirt. Now she laughed. "Don't stop on my account." She crossed the kitchen and put her books down on the table. It was a big, impressive pile. Holly's a sophomore at Merriman College, just a few miles away from where we live.

"Where's Mom?"

I shrugged again. "Out on a job, I guess. I just got home."

"Well, I suppose we should start dinner."

Sometimes Holly is just like another mother. "I have to do my homework first," I said as I sat down at the kitchen table and ripped a piece of paper from her notebook.

Holly started getting out food, banging drawers, rinsing vegetables.

Quickly I wrote:

> The kitchen is a pleasant place.
> It makes a smile come to my face.
> And even if there are dirty dishes there,
> I'm glad to relax in a kitchen chair.

Yuck! I thought. How could I ever be a poet when I wrote trash like that? Well at least it was a start. Mr. Manson always said everything needs a place to start. I had to begin thinking of myself as a poet, change my image. Being just a plain old, medium-cute high school sophomore wasn't enough anymore. "Who's a good poet?" I asked Holly, who was now peeling potatoes.

"That's a weird question from you." She flipped potato skins into the sink. "Assignment in English?"

"Yeah. Sort of."

"Well," Holly said, "how about Robert Frost?"

I shook my head. "It has to be a girl."

"The most famous woman poet is probably Emily Dickinson."

"Emily *who*?"

"Dickinson." Holly giggled and nodded toward her books. "Look her up. We just read some of her stuff in my lit class. She was from Massachusetts. Not too far from here, actually."

There were five poems, all short, listed under Emily Dickinson's name. I read one out loud.

> "Hope" is the thing with feathers—
> That perches in the soul—
> And sings the tune without the words—
> And never stops—at all—

"Weird," I said. "Emily is really weird."

"Was," Holly corrected. "She's been dead for more than a hundred years. And you're right, she was weird. She was always alone and always wore a white dress."

"So why read stuff a dead person wrote?" I asked. *My* poet was much more interesting. He was alive.

Holly rinsed the potatoes and tossed them into a pot. "Emily Dickinson was a great poet. Her poems will probably be read and loved forever."

I read the poem again. " 'Hope' is the thing with feathers . . ." What could that mean? I looked over at Holly. "Did Emily Dickinson have a bird named Hope?"

Holly shook her head and looked at the ceiling.

I played with the idea of being like Emily Dickinson. I liked it. I could picture myself sort of drifting, alone, between classes at Newton High. *There goes Ann Margaret*, they'd all say. *The poet. She's friends with that other poet, Padraic McKinnon.*

When people talked to me, I'd answer back in a lilting, poetic voice. And I'd memorize all kinds of quotes from famous poems to throw into my conversation. "I am going to be a poet," I told Holly.

Holly shrugged. "Well, I guess that's better than being a cheerleader. It's quieter anyway."

Why didn't people take me seriously? "I already have a *mentor*," I shot back, not smiling. "A famous poet who will guide me to write great things."

Holly didn't hear the last part because she'd turned on the garbage disposal. "Why is my sister such a pain?" I asked the napkin holder. "It would be much easier to grow up with a sister who was mature and understanding."

"Come on!" Holly said when she flipped off the disposal. "You're supposed to be helping."

I stood up, putting my hand over my heart. "I think that I shall never see, a peeled potato fat as thee."

Holly rolled her eyes. "I can't stand it. You'd better go back to wanting to be a cheerleader."

Mom stood in the doorway, eyeing my room, where I'd retreated to write a poem about love and a shoe. "Your wallpaper looks a little faded. Are you getting sick of it?"

"No." I jumped up from my desk. "No thanks." That look in her eyes made me nervous. If I agreed, she'd attack my room with her ladder

13

and wallpaper steamer, oozing glue onto my floor. "It's fine. Really, I love it." I smiled at the tiny-rosebud print wallpaper, the oak bookshelves crammed with stuffed animals and pictures of my friends, and the bed with its fluffy pink quilt that hung down to the polished floor. I swung my arms around. "I love my room." It had only been six months since she'd redecorated the last time, and it had taken her weeks. I wasn't ready to go through it again. "I thought you were busy."

Mom nodded as she examined my curtains. "I guess I'm just looking for something to do to console myself if I don't get the Howland House. You know that big house the historical society owns? They just got a government grant, and they're going to restore and redecorate." She sighed, staring out the window. "I bid on the job today, but I'm sure they'll give it to Arpell's in Boston."

"Why?" I asked. "You're just as good."

"Yes." Mom turned away from the window and grinned. "And I bid low, too. So if I get the job, I'll have to hire cheap labor." She started out of the room, then turned and called over her shoulder, "You don't mind, do you, honey?"

She was gone before I could answer. "Rats!" I said loudly. "Poets don't hang off ladders painting ceilings." Why did everybody see me as someone different? Tommy saw me as a basketball player. Holly saw me as a dumb little sister. Now Mom wanted to turn me into cheap labor.

I looked at myself in the mirror. I needed isolation if I was going to write poetry. I needed to contemplate life, the world, the universe. I had to think about important things like love.

Lost in thought now, I pictured a lifetime stretching before me. Publication in important magazines, honors, prizes. I would give speeches at places like Harvard and Yale. People would lean forward to listen to every word I said. They'd quote from my poems. And Padraic would be there in the audience—adoring and admiring. I giggled out loud at the thought, then frowned. That certainly wasn't a poetlike giggle.

Chapter Three

"You're going to ruin your life," Barb said on the phone later. "I've been thinking about it, and I think you should give him up, Annie. He's way too old."

I flopped on my bed. "You already told me that, remember? All the way home from school."

"It's for your own good. I don't even care if you get mad."

I stuck my legs straight up, staring at them. "My tan's almost gone. We worked all summer sweating and burning to get gorgeous tans, and you should see my legs now. Yuck. I've got pale turkey skin, and it's only October."

"Don't change the subject." Barb spoke sternly. I could picture her sitting on the edge of her water bed, floating gently as she talked. "He's cute and it's neat that he's a poet. But he's way too old for you."

"Age doesn't matter," I told her defiantly. "Neither does cute. Your mom's a psychologist. Ask her."

"Annie, you have to be yourself. You keep

trying to be someone else. Anyway, since when have you liked poetry?"

I sat up and traced the pattern of the braided rug with my big toe. "I am being myself, Barb," I said in my most serious voice. "I'm just discovering parts of me I didn't know I had before. Hidden talent and stuff."

I stretched to see myself in the oval-framed mirror. "Just wait," I said. "I'll be famous. You'll be proud to say you knew me when." I pushed my hair back from my face, Emily Dickinson-style, and practiced frowning. "I have to go so I can write my poetry. Farewell, dear friend."

I hung up and decided to go outside. I thought if I got a little exercise, a poem would come to me.

I went downstairs to the garage and got the basketball. I'd start with that, I thought as I went out to the driveway. I began to tap out a rhythm with the ball, then put words to it, sort of like writing a song. *Tap, tap, tap, bong. Tap, tap, gong.* Then I took a shot at the net over the garage door.

I was repeating the tap-tap-taps under my breath when Tommy came out.

"Hey, where'd you go this afternoon?" he asked as he came up behind me, stealing the basketball. He bounced it a few times and swished it through the net.

"I had some stuff to do," I told him, falling into the game, dribbling the ball around the driveway.

"Yeah, I saw you stop and talk to that weirdo." Tommy lunged for the ball just as I got a shot off.

"What weirdo? I didn't talk to any weirdos." I grabbed the ball as it bounced, and faked, turning one way, then another.

"That poetry guy. You know, the one with the lipstick on his wineglasses and the weeds in his lawn."

"He's not a weirdo," I snapped back, dribbling around Tommy, then going in for a lay-up. "He's a very prestigious poet. So there." I put my hands on my hips and let the ball bounce across the driveway. "You have no class if you don't appreciate good poetry."

Tommy shrugged, watching the ball roll until it caught in the grass. "I'd rather play basketball."

"Too bad you're so lousy at it," I said, giggling again. I picked up the ball and began to play for real. I dodged, faked, and shot, forgetting about poetry for a while.

"Hey!" Tommy laughed. "You're really hot today. You might even catch up to me. I figure the score is about 10,452 to 8,893—my favor."

"Liar! Hey, how about if the loser tonight pays in ice-cream cones. Big ones."

When we were through, Tommy had lost. We rode our bikes down to Dawson's, where I ordered a double scoop of Chocolate Fudge with jimmies on top.

"Aren't you afraid you'll get fat?" Tommy asked, licking his small vanilla.

"Who cares?" I shrugged. "Surface beauty is not important. It's inner beauty, the beauty of the *soul*, that matters."

Tommy shook his head. "You're getting to be

a real drag. Don't turn weird like that poet, okay?"

"Poets are not weird," I argued between bites. "And Padraic is most definitely not weird. Besides, I plan on being a poet, too."

"You?" He pretended to gag. "Well, I heard most poets drink too much or go crazy." He leaned against the high-backed booth and grinned at me.

"You'll see. Some day you'll brag that you used to know me."

"Yeah, like my dad tells me about how he knew the mayor because he went to school with him. He says the mayor, when he was a kid, stole cookies out of the other kids' lunches. Hasn't changed at all, my father says."

I laughed. I'd known Tommy for too long to let him bother me. He was like a brother, someone to hang out with, to play basketball with. I looked at his freckled face. His rust-colored hair was hanging over one eye. "Hey, know what? Yvonne Smithson thinks you're soooo cute."

He blushed and stood up. "Let's go," he said. "It's getting dark, and I have homework to do."

"Have you ever heard of Emily Dickinson?" I asked when we were almost home.

"Sure."

"Well?" I stopped in front of my house.

"She's the actress who married the baseball player."

"Wrong," I said.

"Okay, okay," he rushed on. "I was only kidding. I don't know who she is."

I sighed. "Emily Dickinson, it just so happens, is the most famous woman poet ever."

"Yeah." Tommy nodded. "That's right. She lives in L.A. and writes movies, too. Real trashy stuff." He laughed.

"You are never serious," I told him. "There comes a time, you know, when we have to grow up, become mature. I bet you don't even know what you want to be."

"You mean when I grow up?" He stopped and picked a chrysanthemum from the bush near our driveway. "I do, too. I want to be happy." He stuck the flower in my hair and smiled. "I want to laugh a lot and enjoy myself. And beat you at basketball."

"Never," I said, shaking the flower at him. "Never, never, never."

That night I came up with a plan. I had to make things happen. I couldn't just dream about stuff. I had to find a way to get Padraic to notice me and think I was special.

The next day after school, I went to the library, where I found four books on Emily Dickinson. If I could just capture that image, I thought, looking at the faded pictures, Padraic would look at me and *know* I was a poet. There was a drawing of her face on the cover of a paperback. Her hair was pulled back into a loose bun, and her chin was tilted up, sort of like a model's. She looked very serious.

Another picture showed her dress on display in some museum. It was a long white shift—prim and proper like a nightgown.

I looked down at my jeans and my oversized sweatshirt. I only had three days to go before my first poetry workshop. That's when I decided to go to Alice's Attique, a secondhand clothing store.

I walked down Main Street lugging my knapsack, now heavy with books about Emily, until I came to Alice's. The little bell jingled when I opened the door.

I took a deep breath and smelled the dusty, musty-attic smell. It was dark like an attic, too. Racks of dresses were scattered around the tiny shop. Old open trunks were filled with folded clothes, and a hanging gold birdcage was used to display old jewelry.

"Hi, Annie dear. How's you mother?" Alice, her white hair tied tight in a braid that wound around her head, sat behind a small counter knitting. Her wrinkled hands were knobby with arthritis, but she still clicked the needles back and forth like castanets. "Your mother looking for something?" Even though she looked up at me, the needles kept going clickity-clickity.

"Oh, you know Mom," I told her, looking through some dresses. "She's always looking for authentic antiquey stuff." It was true, too. Mom bought stuff in Alice's shop that she worked into quilts for wall hangings. She also did fabric pictures, like a country scene of a little girl with pigtails holding a milk can and standing in a green meadow—all of which she'd cut from scraps of Alice's things.

Alice pointed to a rack across the room. "Old Mrs. Berryman moved and brought in a lot of stuff. Lots of nice old dresses. Years ago, before

21

her husband died, they had lots of money. Some of them are barely worn."

I moved over to where she'd pointed. I liked it better when I didn't know the people things had once belonged to. Mom thought it was a compliment to them, though. Sort of memorializing their lives.

I looked through the clothes—an old chenille bathrobe with big flowers on the pockets, cotton housedresses that were faded and thin. Then I saw it—a graying dress made of sheer white cotton. Tiny flat white buttons went all the way down the front. The skirt was full and flattened into the shape it had been in for so many years. The sleeves were long and kind of puffy. I wanted to open my book to the picture so I could compare it, but not in front of Alice. I was too embarrassed.

"That one's quite old," Alice remarked. "Must go back at least fifty years." She squinted at it. "Pretty, though. Throw it in a weak bleach solution, and I bet it'll come out nice and white."

I took it off the rack and held it out. It was too long for me, but it did look like the one Emily wore. It also looked kind of ghostly, too. I decided to get it.

On the way home, with the dress rolled up in my bag, I figured out it had cost about five cheeseburgers and four orders of fries. That's the way I figure financial stuff. It made spending money make sense. At least that was that many more calories I wouldn't eat.

When I finally shook the dress out in my room, I sneezed from the dust. Then I hung it on the oak mirror and opened my book to compare it with Emily Dickinson's dress. Except for the collar and the full sleeves, it looked almost the same. I was glad it was unseasonably warm out so I could wear it. I held it up to me and looked in the mirror. I would remind Padraic of Emily in a subtle, quiet way, I decided. I practiced my floaty walk around my room, then blasted the radio and did a quick cheer for old times' sake.

Chapter Four

By Thursday, I had the perfect Emily Dickinson hairdo to go with my dress. First I pinned my hair into a bun, and then I pulled some strands out so they hung down on both sides of my face. I really looked artistic, like I'd been working on my poetry all day.

On Thursday night I tried the dress on and stood in front of my mirror. It was a little big, but that made it feel more graceful. I practiced walking back and forth across my bedroom floor. I was doing what my mother calls positive envisioning; I was imagining the new me so that my poetic, Emily Dickinson side would be noticed—especially by Padraic.

I imagined how Padraic would look at me. He'd be startled at first. Then he wouldn't be able to take his eyes off me.

On Friday when I woke up, however, I could hear the rain before I even opened my eyes.

"What did Emily Dickinson wear when it rained?" I asked Barb over the phone.

She groaned.

"I'm serious. I have to be authentic. I just

didn't plan on this. Positive envisioning doesn't work on weather."

"If Emily Dickinson was the reclusive whacko you say she was, she probably didn't go out in the rain," Barb said.

"But I have to go to school! Today's the most important day of my life."

"So wear a trench coat over your ghost dress. Maybe the rain'll stop later."

"I guess so."

"Did you finish your poem?"

I sat up in bed. "Don't push me, Barb. I told you—poetry takes time. And concentration. I'm sure Padraic will understand the creative process." I cleared my throat. "See you out front in half an hour. Bring an umbrella."

Things were off to a bad start. First, I had to wear Dad's trench coat because mine wasn't long enough to cover up my dress. Then my hair got wet, so the hair spray I'd sprayed on got sticky and gross as soon as I walked outside.

"Boy, do you look awful," Barb said from under her red umbrella.

"How can this be happening?" I asked, jumping over a puddle. I sloshed along, feeling my feet squish in my white flats.

"The weatherman said it was going to clear up by next week," Barb offered optimistically. "Hey, smile. Poets get wet, too, you know."

"Yeah," I agreed, pulling Dad's coat tighter around me. Nothing was happening the way I'd planned. First, I didn't have a poem to show Padraic. And now, instead of looking like Emily

Dickinson, the poet, I looked like Ann Margaret Thornton, the drowned rat!

When we finally got to school, I shook Dad's coat out before I hung it in my locker. Then I dried my hair as best I could with paper towels from the dispenser in the bathroom.

"Hey, you getting married or something?" Tommy slumped down beside me in first-period history class.

I ignored him and kept staring at the paper in front of me. At the top I'd written LOVE IN A SHOE in block letters and drawn flowers and hearts around it. The rest of the page was blank.

"You really do look like a bride, Annie. Is that dress something new of Holly's?"

"Yes," I finally answered defensively. "These white dresses are the big rage around campus."

"You don't have to be so snobby about it." Tommy opened his history book. "I'm so nervous. I didn't study for this quiz last night, and I can't afford to flunk it."

"Oh my gosh. Me neither." I flipped to the page where Abraham Lincoln's picture frowned back at me. I'd been so busy trying to be Emily Dickinson I'd forgotten about the history quiz.

The whole day went like that. In PE we played volleyball, and Tara Peyton stuck her elbow in my eye going up for a spike. Then I realized I'd forgotten my lunch and had to buy a sandwich in the cafeteria. All that was left was peanut-butter crunch. I figured it was chunky peanut butter, but no. It was peanut butter and grated carrot on some disgusting brownish bread.

"You don't *have* to go to this poetry thing,

you know," Barb said after school, watching me rub makeup onto my face. "Why don't you just skip it? Maybe we can go check out the new supermarket."

I shook my head. "I can't get out of it. Mr. Manson smiled at me in class today. Later he told me he was glad I'd signed up for the poetry workshop." I made a face in the mirror. "I can't afford to have him hate me again."

Barb shrugged. "Want me to come with you?"

"Want to?"

She shrugged again.

"It's okay," I told her. "Emily Dickinson was a loner. I plan on just kind of sitting there staring at him, anyway." I fluttered my eyelashes, and we both giggled.

I'd never been in the classroom where the workshop was scheduled. As soon as I walked in, I knew why. The room was about half the size of a regular classroom, and instead of desks there were four long tables pushed into a square with chairs around the outside.

I stood in the doorway, wondering if I were in the right room.

"Yes, you're in the right place, Annie," Mr. Manson said as he came in behind me. He smiled as I moved inside. "We use this room for teachers' meetings, meetings with parents, some honors classes."

"I have Contemporary Literature in here," one of the four girls at the table offered. She pushed her round gold-framed glasses up on her nose. "It's wonderful," she said. "It's so intimate and cozy. We can really get into the poetry and share our feelings."

A few boys came in. Then a group of five girls.

By the time it was three o'clock and Mr. Manson had left, twelve kids were sitting around the table.

I opened my notebook to my LOVE IN A SHOE page. Half the page was now full of hearts, but I still hadn't written a word.

Then the door opened, and Padraic walked in.

I swear that if my life were a movie, this would have been the moment when the music stops and the audience is left hanging. The moment of impact. Padraic's hair, wet from the rain, hung across his forehead. Under his wet black eyelashes, his eyes were even bluer than I remembered. He wore faded jeans and a rain-wet dark jacket, which he took off. Pushing up the sleeves of his blue sweater, he sat down.

No one said a word.

Padraic cleared his throat. "I'm glad you're all here." I stared at his hands, which held a worn notebook he had brought with him. His fingers moved as he spoke. "I thought we'd begin by introducing ourselves." When he talked, he bent his head forward and concentrated on us. "You want to start?" he asked the girl in the gold-rimmed glasses.

She leaned forward. "My name is Kimberly Simmons." She smiled shyly. "My friends call me Kim."

"Hi, Kim," Padraic answered in a low voice. "Tell us more about yourself."

Her eyes got wide. "I love literature, especially poetry by Dylan Thomas. I've been writing since I was six, and I plan to be a novelist."

"Wonderful." Padraic had a dimple when he smiled. "I'm glad you're here, Kim."

It went like that. As each kid told about himself or herself, Padraic stared at the speaker in the same attentive way.

I smoothed my dress and sat up straight so he could see more of it from where he sat across from me. I tilted my head up when it was my turn. "Hi," I said in my most poetlike voice. "I'm Ann Margaret Thornton."

Padraic nodded. "Yes, I remember. The one who writes love poems about shoes."

The other kids laughed.

I blushed and nodded. He remembered me! "I've been writing poetry ever since I can remember. My absolute idol is dear, dear Emily Dickinson. And I love her bird Hope, too."

Someone giggled.

"I plan on being a poet forever. And I'll live in a big old house with gardens, where I'll go for inspiration."

Padraic was staring at me. *Me!* My Emily Dickinson—me. He'd noticed! My heart was doing somersaults. Could he hear it?

"Emily Dickinson," he finally said, "is my favorite female poet."

I put my arms on the table so he'd be sure to see the sleeves of my dress.

"I love her work," he went on. "I didn't know she had a bird. Whose research did you find that in?"

"Emily said it herself," I answered, a little

29

nervously. "It's in . . . it's in . . . one of her poems," I finished, flustered.

He grinned broadly and kept staring as if I were the only person in the world and he was fascinated by me.

"Do you imitate Dickinson's style when you write?"

I nodded. *And her hair. And her clothes . . .*

"Wonderful," he said softly. "You know,"—he turned his eyes toward the rest of the group—"Ann Margaret has found a great technique. Beginning poets—all writers, in fact—can benefit by finding a poet they most admire and imitating his or her style. That's how you find your own style." He smiled at me as if we were sharing some secret.

Now I was sure he'd noticed I actually was Emily Dickinson. I forced a frown like the one she wore in her picture.

"I'd like you to read a lot of poetry," Padraic went on. "Find a poem you like and bring it to the workshop next week." He stretched his neck to look out the window at the black sky. "The other thing a poet must do is get in touch with his or her feelings. Practice by writing them down the moment you feel them." He paused and looked around the tables at everyone. "Keep a journal just for writing. Carry it with you so you'll always have something to write in."

Everyone nodded. Kim scribbled notes. Outside it was beginning to thunder and lightning.

"Let's try it," Padraic said. "I'll give you a word to write in the middle of a blank page.

Then you write whatever comes to mind about that word."

So this was how it was done. I flipped to a blank page in my notebook. This was easy. I had lots of emotional thoughts.

"The word," Padraic said, "is lightning."

Everyone started writing. I could see them from the corners of my eyes.

I wrote the word down. Then I drew a picture of a lightning bolt that went clear across the page, from corner to corner.

Lightning! Crash!! Kaoom!!! BANG!!! BANG!! I wrote around the edges. *KAZOWIE!! WHAMO!!* I made my letters big to get the full impact of their meaning. Then I made little jagged lines around the lightning bolt like electricity coming out. I did that until everyone else had stopped writing. Kim was the last.

"Okay," Padraic said. "Who wants to share?"

A girl across from me raised her hand. Padraic nodded.

Her voice was soft, quivery.

> Lightning tears across the sky,
> Bringing terror to my eye.
> Remembering each jagged bolt,
> I put my hand against my throat.
> I recall how fear came over me,
> If I were standing beneath a tree.

A few kids giggled. Padraic cleared his throat. "That's very nice, Lucy," he said in his soft voice. "I like the way you captured your feelings about lightning. It's an honest first effort. See

31

if you can rewrite it so it doesn't rhyme. A poem doesn't have to rhyme, although it can."

Then some other kids read singsongy stuff. Kim wrote some weird thing about lightning in her heart. I looked out the window, hoping Padraic wouldn't notice me.

"Ann Margaret?" he finally asked.

I put my hands over my lightning bolt and looked into his blue eyes. "I—I'd rather not share," I told him, looking back outside because I can never look anyone in the eye when I'm not telling the truth. "My . . . my poem is so personal, I'd rather not share it."

Then there was this long minute where no one said anything. Could he tell I was lying?

"I admire your honesty," he finally said. "You seem to already be in touch with poetry. Of course I understand. I hope you'll eventually feel comfortable enough to read for us." He gestured around the table. "I know you've been influenced by Emily Dickinson, but remember that her greatest gift to the world was her poetry, read now by millions."

I nodded. Then I looked down at the backs of my hands. "I'll try," I said in a small voice. "Next time I'll try."

At that moment the door banged open, making everyone jump. I turned around, thankful for the interruption.

"Hi, Annie!" Tommy, a pile of books under one arm and a basketball under the other, burst through the door. "Sorry I'm late." He tossed me the basketball, then closed the door with his free hand. "I wanted to come earlier, but basketball tryouts were today." He turned toward

Padraic and grinned. "Annie's been talking about this all week and since I'm so lousy in English, I figured I could use some practice writing. Annie's crazy about this. She thinks she's going to spend her life being a poet now." He sat down next to Padraic.

"I know you," Kim said. "You're in my Spanish class."

Tommy nodded. He looked around at everyone again, then back at Padraic. "Ever get rid of those dandelions in your lawn?"

Chapter Five

"I wanted to strangle him! Instead I kicked him under the table as hard as I could. I haven't done that since I was ten and he rode his bike into my lemonade stand."

Barb bounced on her water bed, sending out little waves that showed beneath her fake-fur bedspread. "Why did you get so mad? That's not like you."

I paced, digging my toes into her thick carpet. I took deep breaths. "Padraic says we have to be in touch with our emotions. Express them. And those were my feelings," I went on, clenching my fists. "Anger! Hate! I can't believe how he embarrassed me, in front of *Padraic*." I put my hand over my heart for emphasis.

"Oh my gosh. You've got it bad." Barb lay back on her bed and stretched her arms over her head. "I can't believe you want to skip the whole high school experience—parties, football games, going steady—just to fall in love with an older man."

"Look who's talking," I told her. "Who's already collecting college catalogs? Who's all concerned about her grades?"

"That's different," Barb protested, sitting up so fast the top of her bed looked like high tide. "Being interested in college is normal. You have to plan for it in high school. Take the right classes, get good grades." Her voice was getting louder. "You're skipping the whole thing and moving on to a grown man with a career!" She put her hands on her hips. "And it's a lousy career choice, too! How much does the average poet make in a year?"

"That's not important," I told her, picking up my father's trench coat. "Feelings are what's important. Emotions! I came here for sympathy and understanding, and all I get is criticism. You're as bad as Tommy."

"Not quite," Barb said, laughing. "Come on, don't be so sensitive. You're so wrapped up in your own problems you don't even care what happened to me today." She folded her arms and gazed out the window at the rain.

I sighed and sat down. "Okay. You're right. And I'm sorry. I'm just . . . crazed, that's all. What's happened?"

Barb grinned. "He's blond, has blue eyes, and he's tall." She hugged herself. "Adorable even! And he smiled at me."

"At you?"

"Yeah. When I went through his line with my loaf of bread."

"You went to the new supermarket?"

Barb nodded enthusiastically.

I stood up. "How can you think a bag boy is more important than a poet?"

Barb rolled her eyes. "Because the bag boy is sixteen, that's why. And his name is Todd. I read it on his name tag." She grinned. "Will you go there with me after school next week?"

"Sure." I sighed. Loudly. All poets sighed, didn't they? I sighed again. "I have to get home. Padraic says we have to write our feelings in a journal. So I'm going to try writing this stuff down. Since my friends aren't interested . . ."

Barb threw a pillow at me as I went out the door.

"Hi, hon!" Mom yelled from the kitchen as I unlocked the front door.

I came inside and stood in the doorway, watching her study paint samples at the table. "You're home early."

"That I am. Mrs. Long's dining room is finished, so I left early." She paused. "Tommy called three times, at least. He must've forgotten his homework or something. He sounded upset."

"Good." I slapped my hand on the table. "I hope he stays upset. I don't ever want to talk to him again."

"Oh?" Mom looked up and frowned. "Why? I know you two haven't been playing basketball lately. Is there a problem?"

I stood up. I was sick of talking about Tommy. "He's just immature, Mom. I've outgrown him. He came to my poetry workshop and embarrassed me. I wanted to die right there. I just left quietly as soon as the workshop was over."

"Oh?"

"Yeah. When he calls back, I'm going to hang up on him."

During the next hour, I did exactly that—hung up on him at least ten times. In the end I only talked to him because Mom got tired of the phone ringing every five minutes.

"I don't want to talk to you, Tommy," I told him. "My mother is making me. What do you want?"

"I want to know why you're mad. I want to know why you ran off after that poetry thing."

I groaned. "That's how insensitive you are. You embarrassed me, Tommy. You embarrassed me so much I don't want anyone to know we were ever friends." I slammed the phone down.

When it rang again, I was ready. "This is to inform you," I said, not even saying hello, "that no one in this house wishes to speak to you ever again. Is that understood?"

There was a pause on the other end of the line. Then a snobby woman's voice said, "Am I to understand that you are no longer doing business as an interior decorator?"

I gulped. "Sorry, this is not who you think. This is her daughter—but she's here! I'll go get her." I raced downstairs. "Mom! Mom!" I slid to a stop at the kitchen doorway. "Mom, I'm really sorry, but I thought it was Tommy on the phone and you know I'm really mad at him, so I wasn't very nice and it was this lady who wants you to . . ."

Mom glared at me as she got up to answer the phone.

I ran back upstairs to hang up the phone in my room. Then I spread my books on my desk to make it look as if I'd been studying. When Mom saw that I was working hard, maybe she wouldn't be so mad about what I'd said to her potential client. When I heard her coming up the stairs, I quickly leaned over my science book.

"Annie! You'll never guess who that was!"

Oh no, I thought. I turned around slowly. Mom was grinning.

"I got the job! I got the Howland House!" She spun around my room, then hugged me. "Do you believe it? Do you know what this means?" She swung her arms around. "I can't wait to tell your father. This is so exciting." She kissed my cheek. "Get dressed. I'm taking everyone out to dinner. I'll call Dad at work." She skipped out of the room.

The Red Fox is a fancy restaurant near the Ogunquit Golf Club. I'd been there for lunch, but never dinner. It was very elegant, with flickering candles, white tablecloths and red linen napkins on each table, a deep red plush carpet, and waiters dressed in tuxedos.

Outside the window near our table, lights shone through the rain onto the grassy golf course.

Even at dinner I practiced my poetry techniques. I kept asking myself how I was *feeling*, but after a while I wasn't sure. I was happy for Mom, jealous of Holly for being so smart and pretty. And Dad and I were just being silly. How could I write about all those feelings? I never felt just one way. Was that normal?

"So, Annie," Dad said, turning to me. "You going to work for Mom?"

"Huh?" I squinted at him across the table. "What?"

"You remember, dear." Mom reached across

38

the table and patted my hand—I hate it when she does that. "Remember I said I'd need your help if I got this job?" She took a sip of the champagne Dad had ordered for the two of them. "I'll pay you, of course. We'll have fun together."

I put down my fork. "Mom, I don't want to work for you. I'm a poet."

Dad laughed. "A poet? What's this all about?"

"It happened while you were out of town, Frank," Mom explained.

Holly giggled. "Tell him how you're going to be a poet and get rich and famous."

Dad raised his eyebrows. "You mean a real poet, like Longfellow?"

I nodded.

"A new Emily Dickinson." Holly giggled.

"So what if I am?" I defended myself. "It's better than being an electrical engineer like you're going to be, Holly." My voice got louder. A few people turned to look at me.

"Sh-h-h." Mom frowned.

"That's great, honey. Really," Dad said in a calming voice.

Mom smiled. "And I'm sure you can find some time to help me out. Poets need spending money, don't they?"

"You don't understand," I told them. "I have to live the life of a poet. That means isolation. I need time to contemplate."

Mom and Dad looked at each other.

"Okay, dear," Mom finally said. "We'll talk about it later."

I looked down at my plate and tried to imagine Emily Dickinson scraping paint off a front porch. It didn't work.

"Don't pout, Annie," Dad said. "Let's not spoil Mom's celebration."

"I'm not pouting." I tilted my chin up as high as it would go. "I am thinking about poetry."

Holly giggled again.

"Well, excuse me!" I jumped up, bumping the table and tipping over Holly's ginger ale.

"Great," she hissed as I stood there, mouth open. "It went all over me." She brushed at her dress with a napkin.

"You two go to the ladies' room and clean that up," Mom said in the low, even voice she uses when she's about to get really mad. "And you, Annie," Mom added as we left, "try to control your temper next time, all right?"

My temper! I thought, making my way past the other tables. How unfair could you get? I'd decided to do something important with my life, and all I was getting was abuse!

In the ladies' room, I splashed cold water on my face while Holly sponged away at the soda spots on her dress.

"I don't believe how you can make me act like a little kid again," she told me. "I was having a nice relaxing *adult* dinner, and you had to start a fight."

"See you back at the table," I said sharply. I pushed my way out the door and wound around the restaurant, taking the long way back to our table. By mistake I turned left and ended up in the cocktail lounge.

It was really dark in there. People were sitting at tiny little tables in front of a huge, long bar with mirrors behind it.

It was kind of interesting. I'd never been allowed in a bar before, except once when we were waiting for a table at another restaurant. A cocktail waitress wearing a short black dress came over to where I stood. "Would you like something to drink?"

I shook my head. "No thanks. I was just on my way back to my table." Carefully I made my way across the back of the room, concentrating so hard on seeing in the dark that I was startled to suddenly feel a hand on my shoulder. "Ann Margaret?"

I froze for an instant, then spun around.

"I thought I recognized you." Through the dimness, like a light in the darkness, Padraic McKinnon smiled down at me.

I put a hand down on the chair beside me to keep from shaking.

"I thought you'd be home writing." He smiled.

"I'm practicing what you talked about," I told him. "You know, spontaneous writing. Capturing my feelings." I looked around. "In here I feel . . ."

"Stifled?" he finished for me. "And maybe a bit lost?"

I nodded. "Yeah. I'm here having dinner with my parents." My eyes were getting used to the darkness now. I could see that Padraic was wearing a dark suit, white shirt, and gray and navy tie. Not very poetic, I thought.

"I'd be more comfortable outside, sitting under a tree in the rain." Padraic nodded toward a window.

"Hey!" Just then Holly grabbed my arm. "Where are you going? Did you get lost?"

I frowned at her. Did everyone want to ruin

my chances with Padraic? First Tommy, now Holly . . .

"Who's this?" She nudged me, then turned her attention to Padraic.

"This is my poetry teacher, Padraic McKinnon." I looked at him to see how he would react to my sister. "Padraic, this is my sister, Holly."

Padraic merely held out his hand. "How do you do?"

"Hi." Holly smiled. "So you're the one who's influenced Annie to become a poet and give up her normal life." She shook his hand. "You can't imagine how she's driving us crazy—"

"My sister and I," I interrupted, pushing Holly aside, "have been estranged for some time."

Holly opened her mouth to protest, but I rushed on. "She has problems. You know." I nodded madly, as if I were sending Padraic some secret message. "I'm sure you understand. It was nice seeing you." I grabbed Holly's hand. "Bye, see you Friday." Then I pulled her after me as I left.

Padraic put his hand up in farewell.

Holly pulled away but followed me anyway, complaining as she went.

"Now I know why Annie wants to be a poet," she told Mom and Dad when she sat back down.

Mom and Dad looked up from the chocolate cake they were sharing.

"I just met her teacher," Holly said in a loud whisper. "He's absolutely gorgeous, even in the dark." She nudged me. "Isn't he, Annie?"

I folded my hands and gritted my teeth. "For an older sister," I said, "you are a total embarrassment. The attraction I feel for Padraic is that of a student toward a great teacher. I really admire his talent."

"Sure." Beside me, Holly burst into laughter. When I looked over at Mom and Dad, they both joined in, too.

I didn't wonder about my meeting with Padraic until I was back home in my room. What was my teacher doing at the Red Fox, the most expensive restaurant in town? Why wasn't he at home in his cold garret, writing poetry? Poets weren't supposed to hang out in expensive cocktail lounges, were they? He must actually make money by writing poetry, I figured. Lots of money.

I was so involved thinking about that, I forgot to even try to write a poem that night.

Chapter Six

It was Saturday morning. I couldn't believe I had let Mom rope me into spending a Saturday working on the Howland House, which she was renovating for the historical society. True, it was dreary and rainy out, but I'm sure I could have found *something* better to do—like practice writing my poetry. I really had to get going on that if I ever wanted to impress Padraic. I still hadn't been able to write a single poem!

Mom had hired Barb and Tommy to help us for the day. At first I was mad when she told me about Tommy, but I had to admit that it was nice to have his help—and his company—around the big old house. Rumor had it that the last Howland who had lived there had murdered his wife. When we were younger, the three of us had believed the house was haunted; on dark nights we used to dare each other to go up to the windows and look inside.

Even this morning when we caught our first glimpse of it through the rain and fog as we drove slowly up the long drive, Barb and I shivered. The Howland House, which had been built in 1769, was dark and full of shadows. The white clapboard had turned a dull weathered gray. Pine needles and overgrown weeds covered the walk. It wasn't hard to believe once again that it could be haunted. When Mom fit a large, old-fashioned key into the lock and the front door creaked open, I was glad to have Tommy there. With him clowning and joking as usual, I forgot to look for ghosts around every corner.

I hadn't totally forgiven Tommy for embarrassing me in front of Padraic, the one person I really cared about impressing. But it was hard to resist his infectious good humor.

I groaned with distaste as I gathered up an armful of garbage and stuffed it into a big plastic bag. It's one thing to clean your own room, but renovating an old house that no one has lived in for ages is a million times worse! Over the years, before the house was boarded up by the town, people had broken in, leaving behind old newspapers, now yellowed and dusty, broken bottles, and old tin cans. The floor was littered with twigs and pinecones where the wind had swept them in through broken windows or cracks. And there was just plain dirt on everything.

"So you're not mad at me anymore?" Tommy asked when Mom and Barb had left to start in on another room.

I tried to glare at him but it didn't work. "No." I shook my head. It was hard to stay mad at Tommy when he looked at me that way—hurt but trying not to let it show. "But I still don't understand why you came to the poetry workshop when you didn't really want to be there. You knew it was special to me."

For a moment he was quiet, bundling newspapers and stuffing them in a trash bag. "I told you, I need help in English."

"Why weren't you worried about it before?"

He hesitated, concentrating on the floor. "Because I wasn't trying out for the basketball team. I need to keep my grades up to get on the team."

"Oh." I shuffled papers on the floor with my foot. That did make sense. Basketball practice had just started. "And you didn't mean to embarrass me?"

"Of course not!" Tommy shook his head. "I would never do that to you on purpose."

"Well, do me a favor." I picked up the broom. "Don't tell Padraic anything else about me, okay?"

Tommy nodded solemnly.

"The stuff I tell you is private. I didn't think you'd blab it like that."

"Sorry, Annie. Friends?" He stuck out his hand.

"Friends." Then we both laughed at the soot and dirt on our hands as we shook.

"I know what my mother would do with this place," Barb said a while later when she joined us to tackle another room. "She'd clean it all out, knock out those little windows and put in big picture windows, paint all the rooms and ceilings white. Even the fireplace. Then she'd cover the whole floor in eggshell-colored wall-to-wall carpeting."

"Me, too," I agreed. "I'd fill it up with furniture like yours—all black and chrome. Maybe a little glass."

"Great!" Tommy added, getting into it. "We can hang those strings of beads in the windows—the purple, glittery ones. And big pink plastic flowers for decoration." He pointed at the wall with the dustpan. "And mirrors, big mirrors. Mirrors everywhere."

"You're making fun of me, Tommy," I said.

"And my mother," Barb added.

"No, I'm not," he said. "That modern stuff just wouldn't go in here, that's all." He looked around. "I kind of like all the wood. And it has this feeling of—"

"Of being old," I finished, grinning at him.

Tommy shook his head. "No, of being more real. You know—solid, dependable. Traditional."

"He sounds like an ad for Connecticut Manor Furniture," Barb said.

I nodded. "Bor-ing."

"Boring? How can you call this boring?" He threw his arms up. "This old house is exciting." He grabbed the broom away from me. "Think of all the life that's been lived in this room. All the romantic scenes in front of that fireplace!"

Barb groaned. "He's off again."

"Darling," Tommy said to the broom, which he was holding upside down now. "The battle was difficult. The British just wouldn't give up. I loaded and reloaded my musket until my arms ached. The only thing that kept me alive was the thought of you, dear Esmerelda. And of our lovely homestead." He swung around with the broom. "And of course, our loyal Nelly, who's asleep in the barn."

"Oh my gosh. He's really flipped this time," I teased. "Who's Nelly? Your girlfriend?"

"My horse," he informed me, then focused his attention again on the broom. "I've been longing for the moment when the two of us could be alone like this." He moved closer to me and put one hand on my shoulder. "Would you care to dance, my darling?"

I started to laugh, but Tommy continued to stare intently at me. Confused, I dropped my eyes to the floor. "N-no, I d-don't think so," I stammered. I couldn't believe I suddenly felt this tongue-tied in front of my old pal.

He squeezed my shoulders and leaned forward. I thought he was going to speak, but he hesitated, then quickly kissed my cheek.

I felt my face go hot. "Bashful, my dear?" he asked, resuming the old-fashioned speech of his game. "Never mind—I'll just practice until you're ready."

He held the broom at arm's length and began dancing, waltzing and bowing around the shrouded, dusty furniture.

I breathed a sigh of relief. He *had* only been kidding. For a moment I'd thought . . .

"Hark!" I said, deciding to join in his game. "I hear horses' hooves! Who could that be?"

"The British, coming to get even?" Barb giggled. "Or did Nelly get loose?"

Tommy stopped, putting his hand to his ear. "It is . . . yes, it is." He ran to the door and creaked it open, then shut it again. "Why it's my dear neighbor from far away. Dear, dear Emily Dickinson." He looked at me, then back to the door. "Your dearest, dearest friend."

"Emily didn't ride a horse," I said in my normal voice. "And she wasn't born until 1830."

"Ah, but in the night, when everyone else was asleep . . ." Tommy whispered, ignoring the time difference, "she did all sorts of things. And she *loves* this house. Don't you, Emily?" he asked the broom, who had now turned into Emily Dickinson.

"She'd love it better if it didn't get her white dress all dirty," Barb said.

"Emily doesn't mind. Do you, Emily?" Tommy grinned at us. "This house inspires her, she says."

"Ask her if she'll inspire me to write a poem," I blurted out, then put my hand over my mouth. I'd given away my secret.

Barb and Tommy both looked at me.

"I thought you were a natural poet," Tommy said, dropping his act.

I laughed. It sounded hollow and phony. "I'm just kidding. Of course I can write poetry." I walked over to the window. The sun had come out, sparkling down on the wet leaves. "This is all I have to do." I pointed outside. "Just get in touch with nature. Then the words just roll out," I lied.

"Uh-huh," Barb said in a skeptical tone.

Tommy didn't say anything. He just looked at me intently.

49

"What's going on?" Mom called, coming to the rescue. "The place looks great. Want to get cleaned up and go get a pizza?"

"If you insist," Tommy said. "I thought we'd stay here and cook up some wild-pheasant stew."

When Mom dropped us off at Pizzaman's, we were exhausted. "My arms ache," Barb said, plopping down in a booth.

"Me, too," I agreed, sitting down beside her. "Here, Tommy." I handed him the money Mom had given me. "Will you order?"

"What lazybones," Tommy joked. "Pepperoni and sausage okay?"

I nodded.

"And diet colas," Barb called after him as he headed toward the counter. "Large, cold diet colas."

"Let's ask my mom for a raise," I said, leaning back against the seat.

"Or a week's vacation someplace like Florida."

"We'll go when I get rich." I sat up straight, remembering I hadn't told Barb about Padraic being at the Red Fox. Leaving nothing out, I explained what had happened the night before. "See," I finished triumphantly, "poets *can* get rich."

"I think your poet is too mysterious," Barb said. "I think you need to find out more about him." Barb spread her hands on the table, examining her new, long acrylic nails. She'd had them done that morning on a whim at the salon I'd wanted to go to before I'd decided to become a poet. She wiggled her fingers. "Do you think they look okay? I wanted to do something different to myself. I thought I'd be used to them by now, but they still feel kind of weird. And they get in the way."

I touched one, frowning slightly. I did like them, but I didn't want to admit it, even to Barb. I was a serious poet now.

Barb smiled. "I wonder if Todd's working today. If I'm going to take these things off, I have to at least let him see them first."

I leaned back and sighed heavily. "We all have our problems."

"I know. It's awful that you haven't been able to write a poem yet."

I sat up straight again. "I didn't say that."

Barb shrugged. "It's better if you talk about it. At least that's what my mom says. They call it writer's block."

"Writer's block?"

"Yeah. It means your thoughts are blocked and you can't write."

I sprinkled some pepper on the bare table, then pushed it around with my finger. "What's the cure for writer's block?"

"I don't know. Want me to ask my mom?"

I shrugged. "I guess so. It's not that I can't write, you know. I just don't have the time. There's school, and homework . . . and my mom's always got stuff for me to do. Like today, for instance. A poet needs isolation. Time to concentrate." I shrugged again. "My house is just so crazy, between the phone ringing and Holly's loud music."

"I've got it!" Barb grinned. "I know just what you can do!"

51

I looked at her, skeptical.

"Move up to your attic." Her eyes were sparkling with excitement. "Don't poets always do that—go off somewhere to be alone so they can contemplate and stuff?" She looked smug. "Your attic's perfect. It's dark, shadowy, and depressing."

I brushed the pepper into my hand and dumped it in the ashtray. "Maybe you're right." I thought about our attic. It was musty and hot. The ceiling was the inside of the roof, covered with open, bare boards that went up to a high, shadowy V. Mom had all kinds of stuff stored in boxes up there, like Christmas ornaments and old baby clothes. "But it's kind of creepy."

"That's what you need," Barb retorted. "That'll keep you in touch with your emotions."

I thought some more, tapping my fingers on the table. I was still thinking when Tommy came back to our table. Beside him was Kim Simmons.

"Pizza's ordered." He sat down and slid over, making room for Kim. "Look who I found, Annie—a fellow poet."

Kim pushed her round glasses up the bridge of her nose and smiled.

"Hi, Kim," Barb said. "I didn't know you were in the poetry workshop, too." She turned to me. "Kim and I are in algebra class together."

I smiled stiffly. Why did Kim make me feel inferior? "So what are you doing here all alone?" I asked her.

Kim curled her straight brown hair behind her ear. "I just got off the bus from Addington.

There was a one-act play by Marian Robles up there. Do you know her work?"

She was so smug and conceited, I decided as I shook my head.

"She writes poetry, too," she went on. "Padraic introduced me to her work."

"Padraic?" I leaned forward, suddenly interested.

"Sure." Her eyes got wide behind her glasses. "He's wonderful, isn't he? He knows everyone who's anyone in the literary world." She leaned back. "And he was right—the play was great. When I saw him there today, I told him."

"You saw him? Today?"

"Sure. He lives in Addington. And he's Marian Robles's friend. He introduced us after the performance."

"He's such an inspiration," Tommy added, his eyes twinkling. "We're so lucky to be working with him." He stared straight ahead while I almost choked on my soda. I kicked him under the table.

"How well do you know Padraic?" Barb asked.

"Pretty well," she said. "I've heard him read at the Last Word."

"What's that? A computer store?" Barb tried to act interested, but I knew she was just asking questions for my sake. I still couldn't manage to talk with Kim around.

Kim laughed. "You haven't heard of the Last Word?" She looked around the table. "It's really great. It's an old church in Addington that this literary group took over. They do all sorts of neat things there—art exhibits, music recitals, workshops, poetry readings. Padraic reads there every Sunday afternoon."

Barb and I exchanged glances.

"Tommy," Kim said, turning toward him. "Are you going to finish telling me about the novel you're working on?"

"Oh, did he share that with you?" Barb piped in, then looked at Tommy meaningfully.

Kim nodded. "It's exciting, his idea. Isn't it?"

"Oh, yes," I agreed, tongue in cheek. Even in the dim light of Pizzaman's, I could see Tommy was blushing.

"Excuse me." Tommy nudged Kim to get up. "I think I heard my name called for our pizza."

She jumped up. "I'll go with you. I want to hear more about your story."

"I can't believe it," Barb groaned as they left. "She's got a crush on him."

I nodded. "I know. *Everyone* probably has a crush on Padraic."

"No, Annie. She's got a crush on Tommy! I never thought about him being, you know . . . attractive to girls. He's so . . . Tommy."

I nodded. "Yeah, like a brother. He is tall though," I added. "He must be almost six-feet."

"And he does have his license."

I glanced across the room with narrowed eyes to where Kim was leaning on the counter next to Tommy. "We'd better watch out for him, huh?"

"Ha!" Barb scoffed. "Anyone who can make up stories like that doesn't need to be protected. Kim's the one who needs protection."

"Maybe you're right. And anyone who knows

Padraic as well as Kim does wouldn't be attracted to Tommy anyway. Would she?"

"I don't know." Barb tapped her long nails on the table. "All I know is that they're headed back to our table, and she's walking so close to him you'd swear they'd been going steady for years."

I turned and watched. Kim was wearing a long swishy skirt and black sweater, and Tommy, my old buddy, was balancing the pizza between them as he watched her intently.

Suddenly I didn't feel hungry anymore.

Chapter Seven

"I've made an important decision." I was sitting at the supper table Monday evening, looking at Dad and Mom. "A decision that will affect my whole life."

"It's the poetry thing again, I'll bet," Holly said.

I ignored her and went on. "I've been reading about Emily Dickinson, the poet."

"We know she's a poet," Holly said.

"Emily wrote her poetry in isolation. She cut herself off from the cares of the world and dedicated herself to her art." I paused for emphasis. That was a line from one of those literary books, and I thought it sounded good.

Dad raised his eyebrows.

"So my request is really simple. I—" I paused and blushed. "I'd like to move up into the attic." Quickly I looked down at my plate, then stuffed my mouth full of mashed potatoes.

No one said a word.

Mom cleared her throat. "Have you been up there lately, hon?"

I shook my head. "Not since we put the Christmas decorations away last year." When I looked up, I saw Mom and Dad weren't upset at all. Both of them had silly expressions on their faces, as if they were trying to keep from laughing.

That made me even more determined. "It's obvious," I said, "that my family doesn't understand poets. I need isolation to create my poetry. I need to view the world from a special place."

Now Holly laughed. "What a special place," she said, giggling. "Stuck between the trunks and cobwebs."

"Holly," Dad finally said, "stop teasing your sister." He looked at Mom, then at me. "If it's okay with your mother, it's fine with me. I think if you have this desire to write poetry, it will be good for you to follow through with the self-sacrifice it takes to do it well. But your mother worked hard on your room, so if you want to move up to the attic, you'll have to fix it up yourself."

Mom shook her head. "I don't understand why anyone would want to leave a beautiful, authentically restored nineteenth-century bedroom like yours for . . . for an attic." She hesitated. "Maybe I was wrong when we redecorated. Would a little red plastic end table or something modern like that make your room more comfortable?" She swallowed hard, and I could tell this was difficult for her.

I shook my head. "No, Mom. I love my room. And it'll still be my room. Poets need more space, that's all."

"You remind me of Thoreau," Holly said. "Ever hear of him? He went off into the woods and

57

built a cabin so he could be alone and write *Walden*."

I didn't really know anything about him, but I nodded anyway.

"But it was within walking distance of his mother's house, so he could pop in for a home-cooked meal whenever he wanted," Holly added.

"See?" I was surprised at how easy this was. "I only need isolation when I'm working, too."

I finished my dinner quickly, ignoring the looks my parents exchanged. I had to make plans. First, I went back to my room and called Barb.

"I did it," I told her.

"You wrote a poem! Great!" she congratulated me.

"No. No," I replied. "But I took the first step—I got permission to move into the attic."

There was silence at the other end of the phone.

"Barb?"

"Boy," she finally said. "I was only kidding. I didn't really think your mother would let you do that."

"She did. So I'm going up there now to fix things up." I'd propped a picture of Emily Dickinson on my dresser for inspiration. I smiled at her as I talked. "So I'll let you know when I move, okay?"

"Okay." She sounded hesitant. "Annie?"

"Yeah."

"Did you know Tommy asked Kim out?"

"You're kidding!"

"Nope."

I sat down on my bed and kicked my shoes

off. I listened with satisfaction as they clunked on the wood floors. "That idiot. He just wants her help writing a poem, I'll bet. How'd you find out?"

"I talked to Kim in algebra today. She's all excited about it, too."

"Oh, great. Where'd he ask her to go? The movies? Out for pizza?"

"To the dance," Barb replied.

"Wow." I kicked a shoe across the floor. "The dance? The Halloween Howl? The first big important dance of the school year?"

"Yup."

Why was I so mad? I stood up and paced in front of my window. "Why should we care? I mean, Tommy's our friend, that's all. We don't *own* him."

"You're right." Barb said, sounding cheerier. "It's none of our business, so we won't say a word. We won't tell Tommy what a mistake he's making."

"Yes," I said firmly. "It's his life." I took a deep breath. "But you can bet I'll listen really hard to the poetry he writes for that workshop now."

"Yeah." Barb paused. "Maybe he'll start writing love poems to her."

The thought of that made me feel like punching someone. Why did it upset me so much? I kept asking myself after I'd hung up. Tommy had always had other friends. He hung out mostly with the guys who played sports. But then what did Kim, the brainy writer, see in Tommy? She was probably just trying to make Padraic jealous. That was it, I decided. She'd flirt with Tommy in front of Padraic. And then she'd probably even write poems to Tommy that she'd read out loud to the class. I looked at my picture of Emily. "I understand now why you rejected the world. It's full of phonies who pretend to be something they're not. Let Kim and Tommy make fools of themselves. I couldn't care less." *My* poetry that I'd write when I moved up to the attic would be pure. I headed down the hall to check out my new room.

You can tell the door to the attic from the other doors in our second-floor hall because it's narrower. It also has a big old-fashioned key in the lock. I never could figure out why the attic door had a lock. Was it to lock someone up there? Did they lock children up there if they didn't behave? Or maybe that's where George Washington hid his crossing-the-Delaware plans. Anyway, the first thing I did was take the key out of the door and put it in my pocket.

From where I stood in the hall, I could hear the TV downstairs, so I knew Mom and Dad were probably in the den. Holly was on the phone in her room. They were keeping their word—I had to make this move all on my own.

I clicked the light on and went up the steep, narrow stairs, which creaked under each step.

The attic was just the same as I remembered. Cartons and trunks were piled against the walls. A single light bulb on a long wire hung from the rafters, casting shadows on the piles of boxes and old furniture. The floor was wooden. Foil-backed, fuzzy insulation was nailed to the walls and ceiling. "Not very nineteenth-century," I muttered.

By pushing, shoving, and carrying, I stacked the boxes in the back, where the rafters sloped down to meet the floor.

"You okay, Annie?" Mom called up from the bottom of the stairs when I dropped a box.

"Fine, Mom," I yelled back.

"Make sure I can see the labels on all the boxes when you're finished," she yelled up again. "And open the windows. It's stuffy up there."

Mom was right. I pushed open the narrow windows, then rubbed the streaked dirt off the dusty panes.

In an hour I'd cleared a space the size of my room downstairs. Most of the boxes were pushed out of sight. Then I moved the old furniture around so it looked like a real room.

I'd sleep in the old iron bed, and about three old trunks would serve as tables. A broken-down old dresser that Mom had never gotten around to refinishing would be perfect for storage. And there was a huge, rickety desk that would be my writing table. From a carton of miscellaneous pictures, I chose the most depressing ones I could find—black-and-white prints of men in stiff, old-fashioned suits, with bushy mustaches and mad expressions on their faces. I hung them on the nails that were sticking out of the walls. They sort of covered up the insulation in places and gave the room a really serious look. Emily Dickinson would have been proud.

"Oh my gosh. It's Great-uncle Jared!" Holly said a while later, looking at the photos I'd found. She'd just helped me carry the mattress from the extra bed in my room upstairs.

61

"Don't make fun of my new friends," I told her. "This is where I really belong, Holly. I'm home now."

Holly nodded. "You, Uncle Jared, Emily Dickinson, and your creative genius." she muttered as she went down the stairs.

It was almost perfect, I thought, but the mood still wasn't quite right. The bare light bulb was too bright. Suddenly I got a brainstorm. I went downstairs and, with Mom's permission, collected every candle and candle holder she owned —which is lots, considering Mom's taste.

Mom followed me back up the stairs. "You have to be careful of fire, dear. Light only a few at a time, and only use the ones with glass chimneys." She held out a blue ceramic lamp. "This oil lamp works the same as a candle."

She watched as I placed them around my "garret," then lit two on the desk and one on a little pine table next to my bed. Then I snapped off the overhead bulb and smiled at Mom in the flickering light. "It's perfect," I told her. "See? This is all I needed—a place to be creative. Poems will just roll out of me now. I'll just sit at that wonderful old desk and write pages and pages of beautiful poetry."

Mom looked worried, the way she does when she wants to feel my forehead and take my temperature. "I hope your father was right, letting you do this," she said, looking around nervously. "Seen any mice?"

"Mother!" I shook my head.

"Well, if you decide to go back to your room, no one will say a word." She patted my shoulder, still frowning. "I promise."

"Don't worry, Mom. I'll love it up here." I pointed to the brand-new notebook on my desk. "That's going to be my journal. Padraic—you know, my poetry teacher—says we should write in it every day. This will be the beginning of my life as a poet."

Mom nodded again, then started down the stairs. About halfway down, she called back. "There's a program about that new rock group on TV in a little while. Want to watch it?"

I decided to go downstairs to make Mom happy. It wouldn't do to have her worried about me. How could I write with that kind of guilt on my mind? She was so happy she even made popcorn and brought me a glass of diet cola. So I stayed and watched the next show, too, a movie that lasted until eleven. "Oh gosh," I said when it was over, "I let the whole night slip by and now it's so late."

"I know." Mom smiled. "But it was a good movie, huh? I didn't even know you liked Westerns."

I grinned. "That's the first one I've ever seen. And I loved it." I stood up and collected the popcorn dish and glasses. "But now it's so late."

"It is," Mom agreed, straightening the couch. "If I were you, I'd sleep in your own room and save the garret for tomorrow."

I tried to hold back a yawn. "I think you're right. I'm too tired to write. Tomorrow I'll start early."

My room looked strange with the mattress missing from the other bed. And I'd moved all my books, including the ones on Emily Dickinson, up to the attic.

But it felt good, I decided, to snuggle under my familiar covers. And everything would be waiting for me after school tomorrow—in my Emily Dickinson room.

I fell asleep and dreamed I'd won the National Poet's Prize for a love poem and Padraic was the presenter.

Chapter Eight

"I found it." Barb handed me a folded-up piece of paper. "It's a copy of an article from a magazine."

I walked beside her on the way to school, unfolding the paper as I went. The magazine article was entitled, "Unlocking Writer's Block." In a box at the top of the page was a list of rules.

" 'One,' " I read out loud. " 'Get comfortable.' How can I be comfortable when I'm worried about what I'm going to write?" I shook my head. " 'Two: Write in a style that comes naturally.' "

"That means with your hand instead of your foot," Barb said, laughing.

"This is serious," I told her, scowling. " 'Three: Write about what you know.' " I paused. "What does that mean?"

"It means you shouldn't write about love in a shoe unless you've been in love in a shoe."

"Well, everyone wears shoes."

"Does everyone fall in love in a shoe?"

This was exasperating. "You don't fall in love *in* a shoe. You fall in love *with* a shoe."

"Oh. A giant shoe?" Barb giggled.

"Come on. You're just making fun of me." I folded up the magazine article and put it in my book bag. "I'll study it later. When I'm alone and no one will laugh at me."

"Don't be so sensitive," Barb said. "I wasn't making fun of you."

"Yes, you were. Besides, poets are supposed to be sensitive."

Barb and I went on like that all the time, and it never meant anything. We were just comfortable enough with each other to say how we really felt. About everything. I kicked through a pile of leaves. "Seen Todd at the supermarket?"

She shook her head. "Maybe we can go today after school, huh?"

I hesitated. I'd planned on going home right after school so I could go straight to my garret and start writing.

"Okay?" Barb pressed. "I don't want to go by myself."

"Okay," I agreed. "Anything for a friend."

Tommy was sitting quietly at his desk when I got to first-period history ten minutes early. At first I thought he was studying, but when I sat down I realized he was sleeping, his head leaning on his hands over his open history book.

"Wake up. You're in history class."

He looked around, rubbing his eyes. "Yeah. Oh, yeah." Then he grinned at me. "Hey, Annie, how's it going?"

"Fine. How about you? I hear you've been very busy with our little poetry group lately."

He looked confused.

"Come on, don't play stupid. I know you're going out with Kim. You two write poetry together?" *Why did I sound so vicious?* I wondered.

But Tommy didn't seem to mind. "You heard, huh?"

I nodded.

"Kim is a nice girl."

"I'm sure—"

"And she's pretty and intelligent. She's artistic and she has a great sense of humor. She's friendly and everybody likes her. Especially people who like poetry."

"Like you?" I snapped. "How can you say all this stuff? You hardly know the girl."

Tommy looked up at the ceiling. "*She's* easy to get to know. And there's so much—"

I flipped open my history book with a bang. "This is getting sickening. What makes you think I want to hear all about this girl?" I looked down at my book.

"You asked me. Remember?"

I shifted in my seat. "I didn't want her life history."

"You're right," Tommy said. "And I didn't mean to carry on. But there's so many great things about Kimberly. . . ."

I think I would've hit him if Miss Ames hadn't walked in to begin class. As it was, I was so confused by Tommy's glowing admiration of Kim I hardly heard a thing in class.

67

It kept bothering me all day, too. In English class, Mr. Manson picked me to be one of the witches when the class read *Macbeth*, and I really got into it. "Double, double toil and trouble," I cackled. I sounded wicked, just like I felt.

Between classes, I noticed posters for the Halloween Howl plastered all over the school. "Dare to come," read one in the girls' locker room. "The Halloween Howl—rise from your graves and join us. Costumes essential. In ghostly couples or alone." The background was black, with the words printed on shapes of gravestones or ghosts.

"I'm not going," I told Barb after school. We were on our way to the supermarket. "Emily Dickinson wouldn't go to a dance in costume. I don't care who's there, either. I'll be home writing poetry in my garret."

"Well, I'm going to the dance with Todd," Barb said.

"Todd? You don't even know him. You just know where he works and you've seen him around school."

Barb grinned. "I have a plan. Not only will I meet Todd, I'll also find out what his personality's like."

"I can hardly wait," I said in a doubtful tone.

"It's easy. I'll just buy things that will make him wonder about me. You know, arouse his sympathy. Sort of like you writing a poem to attract Padraic's attention." She pulled a list from her pocket. "You'll see."

So for the next three days, we went to the Food Pantry after school. I had to admit Barb's plan on how to capture her guy was easier than mine. But it was also a lot more expensive.

When I saw Todd, I had to admit Barb was right. He *was* cute—even in the red apron he had to wear that said FOOD PANTRY on it. He was tall and very blond.

"I wish he'd look up." Barb and I had squeezed between two newspaper dispensers to peer through the front window at Todd bagging groceries. She took her glasses off and stuck them in her pocket. "Let's go."

That first day she bought bandages, adhesive tape, aspirin, and gauze squares.

When we got to the checkout, she became silent and wore this sad, pained expression on her face. "Oh, thank you very, very much," she said to Todd in a quiet, whispery voice as she held out her hands.

Todd stared for a minute before he handed her the bag, and Barb gave him a weak smile. "Are you okay?" he asked.

Barb nodded weakly.

Outside she squealed with joy. "See? He noticed!"

"What are you trying to do?" I asked as we made our way across the parking lot.

"I'm appealing to his sympathetic nature," Barb said. "He was wondering what was wrong. I've got his attention now."

By Thursday, she'd bought ten boxes of bandages, five rolls of gauze, and a whole closet full of other first-aid stuff.

"Today's the day," she said on Thursday. "Every day he pauses a little longer and looks at me with more interest. Today he'll ask me out." She piled stuff into her cart.

"I'm glad your mother gives you a big allowance." I eyed all the strange little boxes and bottles she'd haphazardly thrown into her cart. "This stuff is expensive."

"He's worth it," Barb said. Today she was limping. While the checkout girl rang up her order, she leaned against the counter as if it were the only thing holding her up.

Slowly the little boxes moved down the belt to get rung up and passed to Todd. One by one, he looked at each item, then at Barb, before he dropped it in her bag.

We all noticed the big pink bottle at the same time—just as Todd picked it up. It was a remedy for chronic constipation!

"Oh, *no!*" Barb almost leapt at Todd, grabbing the bottle out of his hand. "This isn't mine," she said in a too-loud voice. "This must have gotten into my cart by mistake."

They both looked at Todd's hand. A long red scratch ran across the back of his hand.

"Oh, no," Barb said again. "I'm so sorry. I scratched you with my nails." She pulled open a box of gauze and handed him the roll. "I'm really sorry. These nails are new and I have trouble controlling them."

Todd dabbed at his hand. The roll of gauze bounced on the floor, unraveling in a trail of white cotton.

"She's been sick," I told Todd, coming to the rescue. "I mean, you must've noticed all the stuff she's been buying. She's not herself at all. She doesn't usually go around hurting people. She's really a very nice person when she's herself."

The manager came over and leaned over the counter. "It's okay, girls. Todd, take a break and wash that off."

Todd nodded and walked off toward the back of the store, shaking his head as he went.

"Thanks a lot," Barb said when we got outside. "He must think I'm crazy."

I couldn't help it. I started to giggle.

"It's not funny," Barb wailed. "Now he'll never like me. He'll never ask me to the dance. I won't even get to go."

On the spur of the moment, without even thinking, I said, "Of course you will." I was almost crying, too. "I'll go with you. Okay? I promise. We'll both go stag."

Then it hit me. Talk about dumb! Here I was, trying to be a poet, and Barb had me running around chasing bag boys and going to school dances. But the worst thing about going to the dance would be having to watch Tommy and Kim. I was used to Tommy being *my* friend. I wasn't ready to think of him as someone who dated, kissed girls, and fell in love.

That night, for the first time since I'd moved my stuff out of my room, I went up to my attic. It didn't look too bad, I decided, bouncing on the creaky bed.

I lit two candles on the desk, sat down, and opened my journal. Then I closed my eyes and used positive envisioning to imagine myself writing poetry. In my mind I looked like Emily Dickinson, and I had to use a quill pen to scratch out my words.

"Darn," I said out loud, clicking my favorite

ballpoint pen that had little rainbows all over it. "How can I go back for the second workshop tomorrow and still not have written a poem?" I asked myself.

LOVE IN A SHOE, I wrote in big letters on a blank page. Then I underlined it five times.

> Love is a thing with feathers
> that sings and chirps to me.
> That I feel most of all
> when I'm having a ball
> going to the mall
> in my old shoes.

I read it out loud. It was awful. So awful, it wasn't even a poem. I sighed and read it again.

Who was I kidding? I was a boring person with no artistic talent at all. I stared at the picture of Emily Dickinson. "How'd you do it, Emily?" I asked her. Then I tried again.

> Love in a shoe is
> true true true.
> It's not in a tree.
> It's not meant to be.
> It's comfortable, yes
> when you're taking a step.
> It's fun fun fun
> when you want to run.
> It's love in a shoe
> for you you you.

I didn't even have to read that out loud to know it was worse than the one before. I tore both pages out of my journal and ripped them up.

Something was missing. I could feel all my emotions, but I couldn't express them. They were all still scrambled up inside me.

I paced around the attic. I knew what I usually did when I felt like this. I paced some more, thinking of Padraic and how I'd have to look into those blue eyes and tell him I still wasn't comfortable sharing yet. Either that or admit I couldn't write anything worth sharing.

I paced until I couldn't stand it anymore. Then I ran downstairs and clicked on the outside light over the driveway.

In an instant I was outside dribbling the basketball in front of the net. I ran around in circles, dodging, turning, taking shots at the basket. I hadn't played for a while, and I was rusty. I went in for a lay-up. Then I tried a hook shot.

"Hey, can I play?" Tommy's shadow was long and thin across the driveway.

I tossed him the ball. "Yeah. But you're playing the champ here. Can you stand the competition?"

For a while it was like old times. Except Tommy had been practicing.

"Wow," I told him when he made a lay-up. "You keep playing after school, and you might be better than me someday." I bounced the ball down the driveway. "That is, if I decide to play any more."

"Oh, yeah," Tommy said, stealing the ball. "You're going to be a poet and never come outside again." He jumped and made another basket.

I grabbed the ball back and dribbled furiously up to the net. "I don't want to talk about that now."

"Why not?"

I stood there, panting, catching my breath. "Because I don't want to."

He came closer. "I thought you liked poetry. I thought that was all you cared about."

I shrugged. Then, in the light of the streetlamp, I looked into his eyes and I couldn't lie. A fat tear leaked out and slid down my cheek. "It— it's frustrating being a poet." I sniffed back more tears. "It's hard thinking up the right words. And it's lonely, too," I sobbed.

Tommy nodded. Then he moved closer, bending down a little. "It's okay, Annie," he said. "You don't have to cry about it." He came closer, and before I knew what was happening, he put his arms around me and hugged me. Gently, but tight. I could smell the cold fall air in his sweatshirt and feel how the muscles in his chest were hard underneath.

I sobbed again and hugged him back.

"It's okay, Annie," he repeated. "You don't *have* to be a poet. I like you the way you are." Then he bent down and kissed my cheek, like he had in the Howland House.

But it was different this time because he held on. And so did I. We just stood there under the starry sky until I stopped crying.

"You're a good friend," I told him. "Thanks."

He squeezed me again. Then he put both hands on my arms and stood back and looked at me. "When will you learn," he asked, "that you just have to be yourself for me to love you?"

He kissed me again. Only this time it was ever so gently on the lips.

Then he left, running, casting a dark, fleeting shadow across my lawn. He paused for just a moment before he crossed the street on the way to his own house.

I stood there, watching him disappear, feeling the cold wind against my hot cheeks. And the soft, warm place on my lips where Tommy had kissed me.

Chapter Nine

The next morning I felt sick.

"It's that attic," Mom said, shaking the thermometer before she stuck it in my mouth. "You shouldn't have slept up there last night. It's drafty, and it smells bad." She stuck her hands in the pockets of her paint-spattered coveralls. "No wonder you're sick. Want Dad to move your stuff back downstairs?"

I shook my head. Last night had been the first time I'd slept up there. I'd gone inside after Tommy had kissed me, and I'd burrowed under the soft blankets on the bed. And I'd slept. But my sleep had been full of dreams.

Mom took the thermometer out and looked at it. "No temperature." She frowned at me. "Anything going around school?"

I shook my head.

"Any tests today?" Her voice was stern.

"Come on, Mom. You know I'm not a faker."

She patted me on the shoulder. "Why don't you go back to bed in your own room? If you feel better later, you can go to school late. I'll be at the Howland House all day if you need me."

I nodded and went back upstairs, where I stretched out on the bed in my old room and dialed Barb's number.

"I'm sick," I told her.

"That's too bad," she sympathized. "You have to go to school, though. You'll miss your poetry workshop if you stay home."

I pulled the covers up higher. "I don't care. Besides, I don't have a poem."

"What about history class? Annie, you can't miss history today. I thought you were doing badly in that class."

"I am. I'll get the notes from Tommy." My stomach lurched when I said his name. I didn't want to think about him—or what had happened last night.

"You know what my mother would say?"

"What, doctor?" I asked.

"She'd say you were avoiding. When things get tough, people get sick so they can avoid dealing with them."

"But what am I avoiding?"

"Facing Padraic? Writing a poem?"

I paused. "Barb, aren't you going to be late for school?"

After we hung up, I closed my eyes and pulled the covers over my head. That was stupid, what Barb had said about avoiding. Wasn't it? Why would I want to avoid school? I had looked forward to Padraic's workshop all week. And he certainly wasn't putting any pressure on me to come up with a poem.

I lay there until I heard Mom's van drive away and I knew I was alone. Then I got up and took a shower. I'd show Barb I wasn't avoiding anything. All I'd miss was first-period history class—and seeing Tommy.

I pulled on my jeans and a black sweater. Then I pulled my hair back in a tight ponytail and scrubbed my face clean of any makeup. Now I was a contemporary Emily Dickinson—fresh, unspoiled-looking, poetic.

"Let's go around the table," Padraic said that afternoon when everyone was seated, "and each person can tell which poet's work he or she read this week. And maybe tell us something about that poet, too." He had on a deep blue sweater that I noticed matched his eyes. When he pushed up his sleeves, I saw that his fore-arms were tanned and muscular, covered with tiny dark hairs. A sign of masculinity, I thought.

"I'll go first." Padraic smiled. "My poet is Padraic McKinnon. He writes about life, nature, feelings. . . ." He hesitated. "Sometimes love. And he shares observations, absurdities." He looked around the group. "He writes mostly freestyle, short poems, mostly before dawn, when it's quiet and dark."

Maybe that's what he was doing in the Red Fox, I thought—looking for a dark place to write. It was nice to concentrate on Padraic without worrying about what Tommy was liable to say. Maybe, if I was lucky, Tommy would never come back to the poetry workshop.

Next was Sylvia Plath, then Anne Sexton and Adrienne Rich. I recognized them from our literature book.

While each person went on about his or her poet, I practiced positive envisioning on Padraic.

Maybe he would tune into my poetic soul—my anguished poetic soul that cried out to express itself. I made sure the expression on my face was right. Pained.

But my positive envisioning wasn't working. Padraic wasn't supposed to be smiling. He was supposed to be tuning in to my pain.

That's when Tommy came in. "Sorry," he whispered quietly, acting just the opposite of the way he had the week before. "Basketball," he whispered again, placing the ball under the chair Kim pulled out for him. He sat down, ignoring me.

Tommy looked pained. Maybe the torment I meant for Padraic was getting through to him.

"We're sharing poets," Kim told Tommy. "Did you bring the stuff we did at the library?"

Tommy fumbled in his notebook.

"We did our research together," Kim explained. "We chose a couple. A famous poetic couple—Elizabeth Barrett Browning and Robert Browning." Then, in this sickening singsong voice, she read this disgusting poem that went: "How do I love thee? Let me count the ways," which is probably on every stupid valentine ever printed.

"Elizabeth Barrett and Robert Browning fell in love and communicated that love through poetry," Kim explained. "They ran off together to get married and live in Italy." She turned toward Tommy. "Remember?"

Tommy blushed and looked down at his notebook.

"Elizabeth was sickly, but Robert's love renewed her," Kim went on. "When she died, Robert was absolutely devastated."

Finally it was Tommy's turn. He mumbled something about Kim already telling about his poet. Then, in a low voice, he began to read.

Kim smiled madly while he stumbled through this boring poem, "Meeting at Night," that ended with the line, "two hearts beating each to each."

How could anyone be such a fake? I wondered. Tommy was only pretending to be interested in this stuff. He was only using the poetry workshop to make sure he got on the basketball team. Besides, what could he possibly see in Kim? And why had he kissed me when he supposedly liked Kim? Maybe he'd just felt sorry for me.

"Annie," Padraic addressed me across the table. "Do you have a poet to discuss?"

I shuffled the papers in front of me. "Oh, just Emily."

"Ah." Padraic smiled.

"Emily Dickinson was born in Amherst, Massachusetts, in 1830. So she was kind of our neighbor." I grinned. "But she didn't travel much. She stayed in her father's house and wrote poetry until she died in 1886."

"She never got married?" Kim asked.

I shook my head.

"Did she date?" another girl wanted to know.

I shook my head again.

"It's believed," Padraic added, "that Emily was secretly in love."

That sure sounded familiar.

"Her poetry does hint at a forsaken love," he went on. "Don't you think so, Annie?"

I nodded. After all, Padraic knew more about Emily than I did.

"Dickinson spent most of her life as a recluse. Most of her poetry wasn't published until after she died."

"Gosh," one of the boys said. "Imagine spending your whole life doing this stuff and not getting paid or anything?"

"That happens to lots of writers," Kim put in. "Especially poets."

Padraic looked down at the table. Would he tell us now? Would he admit that he had fancy clothes and ate at the Red Fox? Would he tell us how he made pots of money writing poetry? "Money isn't the most important thing in life. I write poetry to express what I'm feeling," he finally said.

I held my hands together. I loved Padraic more now than ever. To be in touch with all that emotion and be able to express it in a poem was wonderful. But I couldn't resist asking, "What about money?"

"Yeah," one of the boys joined in. "Will you ever be able to buy a sports car? I mean, every guy wants a sports car."

"That's not important to me," Padraic said.

"You sound like my mother," a girl offered.

"What'll you drive?" someone else asked.

He laughed. "You all aren't getting any closer to these poets' lives," he said. "Try to understand what it was that made them want to write." He looked back at me. "Why do you think Emily stayed in her father's house and wrote hundreds of poems?"

I shrugged.

"Think about it. Pretend you are in her shoes."

Did he know? Was he telling me in his subtle way that he knew I was Emily Dickinson?

"All of you try it," he went on. "And I have a great place for you to start."

"Where?" Tommy asked.

"They asked me to be a chaperone at the Halloween Howl. I think it would be a great idea if you all came dressed as your favorite poets."

Some kids giggled.

"That's a great idea," squealed Kim. "Tommy and I can come as Robert Browning and Elizabeth Barrett Browning."

"I think I want to come as Mother Goose," Tommy said. "Hey, Annie, do you think Emily knew Mother Goose?"

"I'm going crazy," I told Barb that night on the phone. "I try to get into being Emily Dickinson. I try to take this poetry stuff seriously. Then Tommy makes everyone laugh."

"Why don't you give up on Emily?" Barb suggested. "Bring Padraic some of your mother's chocolate-chip cookies next week. That'll win him over."

I sighed. "You don't understand. I have to get *closer* to Emily Dickinson, figure out why she wrote. Padraic would love me for that." I took a deep breath. "I'm going to Amherst to visit Emily."

There was a long silence on the other end of the line before Barb said, "Have you flipped? How can you visit Emily Dickinson? She's been dead for over a hundred years."

"I'll go to her house and absorb her surroundings. Get in touch with her spirit."

"You really have flipped."

"No, I haven't," I insisted. "That's not crazy. She lived somewhere just off the Massachusetts Turnpike. I just have to get someone to drive me there."

Later, after Barb and I hung up, I paced some more. I wanted to run around the driveway with the basketball, but then Tommy would see me and come out. Instead I took a long, hot shower, then climbed up to my attic garret.

Padraic would get the full benefit of the new me at the dance. I would immerse myself in Emily Dickinson stuff so I'd be just like her.

Then we'd dance. I put my arms out and spun around the attic.

"You do dance well," I said in my Emily voice, which I imagined was high and a little squeaky. "Dear, dear Padraic," I whispered.

We swooped and bowed. It was hard to waltz when I was used to rock stuff, but I managed.

"Sweet, sweet Emily," I imagined Padraic answering as he gazed deeply into my eyes. "You're so . . . poetic."

Chapter Ten

"I took my nails off," Barb said as she climbed into Mom's van the next morning for another day's work at the Howland House. "See?" She waved them in my face.

"Great." Mom grinned. "Now you can scrub floors."

"Tommy coming?" Barb asked as we passed his house.

"No. He called yesterday," Mom answered. "He has basketball practice this morning. Said he'd try to come over in the afternoon to give us a hand."

"That's nice of good old Robert Browning," I said sarcastically.

"Who?" Barb asked.

"Robert Browning. That's his poet. Kim is Elizabeth, his wife."

"Oh." Barb looked as if she hadn't understood a thing. "I like Kim. She's really nice. I talked to her in algebra yesterday. I think she wants to be friends, but she's kind of shy."

"Let me guess—she wanted to know all about Tommy, right?"

Barb looked at me sideways. "So? He's cute. And he's nice."

"Which is more than you're being this morning, Annie," Mom said, glancing at me with a disapproving look.

"You guys don't understand," I told them, settling back. "But you'll see. Just wait'll she dumps him."

Mom had been working at the Howland House for a week, and it really showed. A path had been cut through the weeds to the front door, which looked inviting in the sunlight, its brown wood warm and mellow. The leaves on the tall trees surrounding the house were turning autumn colors of red and gold.

"You didn't see the outside before because it was raining last week. Come look at this." We followed Mom down a little path in the back to the pond.

"I didn't even know this was here," Barb said.

"I think we should get a few ducks," I said. "Liven the place up. White ducks, the ones that quack a lot." I looked around at the thick woods. "It's so deserted. So quiet."

Later, I thought about the house as I worked alone in an upstairs bedroom. Why did people care about these old homes? Why didn't they just tear this place down and build a bunch of ranch houses? Mom would have said something about preserving our history. But why was history so important?

I was on my hands and knees, pulling things out from under a small wooden bed. Acorns, mostly, that squirrels had stored there. Then my hand touched something hard and wooden.

I pulled out an old doll's cradle and stared at it. I set it gently on the floor, and it rocked back and forth. Where was the doll? I wondered. What little girl had owned this? Who had put it under the bed for safekeeping?

Sitting on the floor, I put the cradle in my lap, then turned it over, feeling the old, dry wood in my hands. On the bottom was scratched, in awkward, childlike letters, AMELIA.

"Amelia," I said under my breath. I looked around the tiny room at the wood floor, the plain walls, the small window, and imagined the little girl who had lived there. The little girl who'd played with dolls, just as I had done once.

It was weird. I sat there, sort of connected to Amelia, feeling how similar we were even though we were separated by many, many years.

I wondered if Amelia had ever married and had real babies in real cradles. . . .

"Hi." Tommy, a broom in hand, stood in the doorway.

I shoved the cradle back under the bed. I didn't want to share Amelia yet. She was my special secret.

"Well, good heavens, if it isn't Robert Browning!" I went over and shook his hand. "Fancy you coming here, leaving the little woman. How is Elizabeth?"

For a minute Tommy looked confused. Then he grinned. "She's fine, Emily. She's at home writing a sonnet."

"How quaint. Why aren't you working on your poetry? Or your novel?"

"Now, Emily," Tommy said. "You know I like your poetry better than hers." He came closer, still grinning. "Yours is so mysterious."

"Cut it out, you guys," Barb yelled from the next room. "Get to work! You both sound crazy!" She turned the volume on her portable radio up as far as it would go.

Later, while we were working, I solved my problem about how to get to Amherst. I'd been planning to ask Holly to take me to see Emily Dickinson's house. I was telling Tommy about it when he offered to take me there himself the following day.

"You mean it?" I looked up from the window-sill I was scrubbing.

"Sure." He nodded. "Want to go tomorrow? I know my mom'll let me use her car."

"Oh, uh, yes," I answered. I was about to get up to hug him, but then I stopped. No use bringing that stuff up again. And besides, Kim wouldn't like it.

The prettiest time of year in New England is the fall. I don't know what it's like anywhere else because I've never been anywhere else. But if I didn't have to go to school in October, it would definitely be my favorite month.

As we headed out on the Massachusetts Turn-pike on Sunday morning, Tommy and I got the feeling that everyone else in the world was on a foliage tour through New England. The pike cuts through the center of the state, where the countryside is mostly dense forest. Everyone seemed to be driving slowly, looking at the brightly colored trees.

"That's what you should write a poem about," Tommy said as he pointed out the window. "The fall leaves."

"It's been done."

"So do it again."

I cleared my throat. "Why don't you?"

He was silent for a while. Then he said in this formal voice, " 'Leaves,' by Thomas Fitzgerald:"

When the leaves come down, down, down.
Falling on the ground, ground, ground, ground.
That's when I know, know, know
That soon there will be snow, snow, snow.

I giggled.

"Okay, okay," Tommy said. "Now I'm going to put a tune to it. Then I'll have a song.

"First the drums," he said beating time with his free hand on the side of the steering wheel. "Now the lead guitar!" He made a whining sound in the back of his throat and rocked his head back and forth. "And the lead singer comes onto the stage. Applaud!"

I clapped. "Yay! Yay!"

He started humming a line from a Beatles song. "She loves you, yeah, yeah, yeah . . ." Then he sang his own words to the tune. "When the leaves come down, down, down. Falling on the ground, ground, ground . . ."

I reacted like any adoring fan. I stamped my feet and clapped my hands. "Encore! Encore!" I waved my arms. Then I laughed, and Tommy did, too. I laughed so hard that tears ran down my cheeks and onto the blue turtleneck I'd borrowed from Holly.

"Now it's your turn," Tommy said after we'd calmed down.

I shook my head. "Are you crazy? No way."

"Aw, come on. It's easy," he pressed. "You just take one of your poems and sing it."

I looked out the window. *What poems?* I hadn't written a single one yet. "Let's stop at the next restaurant we pass. I'll treat you to a sundae."

"With nuts and a cherry?"

"With nuts and a cherry."

"Deal." Tommy sat up straighter and tightened his hands on the wheel until we came to a Howard Johnson's.

"Here comes the rock star and his groupie," Tommy said as we walked across the parking lot.

"A groupie?"

"You know, a person who idolizes a celebrity so much that he or she follows that celebrity around. Goes to all their concerts."

I nodded.

"Or poetry readings . . ."

"You think I'm going to a poetry reading to hear that garbage you just spouted?"

Tommy laughed. "I wasn't thinking about *my* poetry reading. I was thinking about—"

I gave him a look. I knew he meant Padraic.

We settled on high, round stools at the counter and ordered our sundaes.

"I'm not Padraic's groupie," I finally told him. "I'm his student. And look who's talking about admiring poets. How's *Kim* these days?" I knew I sounded a little snotty, but I couldn't help it.

"She's probably at home writing poetry," Tommy answered evenly. "While we're out having fun tromping around and eating sundaes," he added in a teasing tone.

"We're not tromping around. We're doing research. It's like a pilgrimage." I took a bite of my strawberry sundae and looked out the window at a majestic, gold-leafed maple tree. "It's more than just a crush on a poet. Poetry's made me think about a whole lot of stuff I never thought of before. It's made me examine my feelings." I looked at Tommy. "That's important stuff. I mean, what good is it to have a brand-new red Porsche if you're lonely? Or if nobody loves you?" I looked back outside. "Or if you don't have anyone to talk to."

"You can always talk to me, you know."

I nodded. "Yeah, I know." I stared out again at the tree, brilliant gold against a clear blue sky. Where had all that stuff come from? I'd been feeling it, but I'd never been able to put it into words.

"Sorry to go on like that," I said as I spooned up the last of my sundae. "I'm really wound up, huh?"

Tommy grinned. "It's okay. Just remember that being happy, even silly, is a real feeling, too."

I rolled my eyes. "Those are so juvenile. I'm talking about important stuff." I suddenly felt shy. "I'll be back in a sec." I went into the ladies' room, splashed water on my face, and brushed my hair. Why was I talking to him about that stuff? I wondered. He'd never understand. Our friendship had changed too much, hadn't it? I'd grown up and gone a different way. Besides, he had Kim now.

When I came out, Tommy wasn't at the counter, so I paid and walked to the edge of the parking lot where he'd left the car. Still no Tommy. I peered into the nearby woods. Sun filtered down in places, lighting the shapes of tree trunks, bushy ferns, clusters of wildflowers, and fallen leaves. "Tommy?" I was sure he was hiding in there.

No answer.

I sat on a rock and stared. A bird squawked, and two squirrels chased each other up a tree. "Okay, fine," I said into the woods. "Make me sit here. I know you're playing games, but it's getting late, and we'll miss Emily Dickinson's house because it'll get dark." I paused and added loudly, "Then I'll hate you forever."

I saw someone move out of the corner of my eye, and I turned to see an elderly couple standing by a car, staring.

"It's okay," I told them. "It's just a game."

The woman looked nervous. Her husband opened the car door as if I were crazy and they had to take cover.

"With a friend," I told them. "My friend's in the woods."

The woman nodded quickly and got into the car.

"Tommy Fitzgerald, you'd better come out now!" I screamed into the woods. "Tommy!" My voice was a shriek.

"Annie, what's wrong?"

I turned and put my hands on my hips. "Where have you been?"

"In the bathroom. What's the matter?" He looked worried. "Are you okay?"

"You weren't hiding in the woods? Come on, you're playing games with me. You were hiding in the woods, weren't you?"

Tommy looked at the woods, then back at me, shaking his head. I could tell that he wasn't lying. But I was still mad. I leaned down, scooped up an armful of leaves, and threw them at Tommy's head. They fluttered down, landing on his hair and shoulders.

He grinned. Then he bent down to pick up some leaves, but I was faster.

I jumped behind him and gave him a shove. Headfirst, he fell into the thick pile of leaves. Then I ran, shrieking with laughter, down the narrow path and into the woods.

"You'll be sorry!" I heard Tommy yell behind me.

I zigzagged off the path and hid behind a bush, squinting through the branches.

"Okay, I know you're here." Tommy ran by, both fists full of leaves. "I'll get you."

I bit my tongue to keep from laughing. Suddenly I had a great idea. First I stuffed my pockets with acorns I picked up from the ground. Then I climbed a tree, a huge elm with wide branches that fanned out over the path. I giggled as I made my way out onto a thick limb. Now I'd just wait.

Straight above me, through the thick branches, I could see irregular patches of blue sky. Tommy's voice got fainter as he wound farther and farther away, until I could hear only the leaves rustling in the cool autumn breeze.

It's so peaceful here, I thought. I balanced myself a little better so I'd be more comfortable. Not bad at all. I closed my eyes and took a deep breath of the moist leaf-and-earth smell of the woods. It reminded me of Robert Frost's poem about the winter woods.

"Annie!" It was Tommy's voice, and it was louder, so I could tell he was on his way back. "Annie! Are you okay?" He even sounded worried.

Crouching down, I held my breath until he came into view and was just below me. Then I let him have it. I pelted him with handfuls of acorns.

"Truce! Truce!" he yelled, jumping away and shielding his face with his arms.

"Not until you surrender," I yelled back, still dropping acorns on his head. "Say, 'Annie is the best and the greatest.' Say, 'Annie is better than me at everything, including basketball!' "

"Okay! Okay!" He waved his arms and ducked behind a tree. "Give me a chance."

He stepped out and looked up at me. "Annie Thornton is the best and the greatest."

This was supposed to be a joke, but he wasn't smiling.

"She's better than me at everything, including basketball. And writing poetry."

I started down the tree.

"And school. Especially at history and algebra," he went on. I was now standing next to him. "And dancing, and being nice and polite, understanding and caring . . ."

"Okay. That's enough." I smiled up into his face, which was flushed from exertion.

"And she's the best, too at making people worry," he went on, ignoring me, "by hiding in the woods so the people who care about her will worry . . . ."

"You knew I could handle myself." I kicked some leaves.

He finally stopped but kept staring at me. "No, I didn't, and I was really worried."

He hung his head, looking upset. I really felt awful.

"I'm sorry," I told him, really meaning it. "I didn't know you'd worry." I took a step closer.

He kept his head down. Then, quickly, he reached out, grabbed me around the waist, and threw me into a pile of leaves. "Ha!" he yelled, scooping up handfuls of leaves and dumping them on me. "Now we're even!"

Chapter Eleven

"How can we visit Emily Dickinson when we're still covered with leaves?" I was sitting on a bench in the town square of Amherst, brushing the twigs and leaves out of my hair.

"I'm sure Emily won't mind," Tommy said. "She's not exactly in a position to criticize."

I gave him a stern look, trying not to laugh. I looked around at the town's center, which looked a lot like every other small town in Massachusetts. We were in the town common, where two main streets intersected. The only streets, I decided. "She's here, in this town." I leaned over and picked a leaf out of the hood of Tommy's sweatshirt. "Can't you feel her?" I closed my eyes. "Just think, she probably sat on this very bench. In this very spot."

"I thought she always stayed in her house."

"She had to come out sometimes." I looked across the grassy square at the town hall, a red brick structure with a clock in its tower. "I can just feel her presence. I really can."

"Will you ask her how we get to her house?" Tommy quipped as he studied the yellow brochure we'd gotten from the man in the tourist information booth.

"Imagine being so famous," I said, touching the paper with one finger, "that your town prints a brochure so tourists can find your house. And they even put your picture on the cover."

"And tell people where you're buried."

I poked him in the arm. "Just you wait. Just you wait till you hear the poems I'll write after I've been here. After I've been immersed in Emily Dickinson's world."

Tommy stood up and put the brochure away. "Her world starts at the Jones Library. That's over there." He pointed across the street. "We can walk to most of these places."

I picked up my journal and camera. I wanted to preserve these moments, to freeze them so I'd remember everything about Amherst. I'd enlarge the pictures and cover the walls of my attic room. I focused my camera on the town hall and snapped. Then I turned and took a picture of the park bench we'd been sitting on.

"You look like such a tourist," Tommy said.

"So do you," I retorted. I snapped his picture just as he stuck his tongue out at me.

The Jones Library was located in a colonial house. Outside it was all gray stone and ornate porches. Inside there was lots of mellow, high-grained wood with hand-carved details. "My mom would love it," I said, standing in the hall.

"Shh." Tommy took my arm and led me up the staircase. "Emily's room is up here."

Why did libraries always feel so serious? I wondered, sliding my hand along the smooth wooden banister. People always whispered and frowned. Books were serious things, I guessed. One didn't joke and laugh in a library. Or at a poetry reading.

When we got there, the Emily Dickinson Room was deserted.

"Where are all the other groupies who come flocking to Amherst in search of Emily?" Tommy asked, following me into the room. It was about the size of a classroom, with books and glass cases lining the walls. In one corner stood a large dollhouse, a replica of the Dickinson home.

"There's her room." Tommy pointed into the dollhouse through the cutaway roof. "Is it like your attic?"

"Sort of," I said. I opened my journal to take notes. The room looked pretty normal to me—a bed, a desk, and bureau. There were pictures on her wall of four stern-looking men. Books lay all over the place.

The glass cases we looked at next held some of Emily's things—buttons, a headpiece she'd worn in her hair, some silverware from her table.

"Imagine," I said, "Emily's fingers actually touched those buttons. The *real* Emily. I wonder if her fingerprints are still on them. Those very hands that wrote all that beautiful poetry."

On the way out, I stopped and bought post-cards, one each of Emily's sister and brother and five of Emily—prints of a portrait I hadn't seen before.

"She looks mad," I told Tommy when we were outside. "Look at her." I pushed the postcard into his hands. "She looks really mad. And she has on a black dress. I thought she always wore white."

I looked again. The black-and-white portrait showed Emily's face. She had large, dark eyes, thick black eyebrows, and a big nose. Her dark hair was parted in the middle and pulled back from her face.

"She's ugly," Tommy said. "Now I know why she hid from people all those years. She got tired of people saying, 'There goes that ugly Emily Dickinson.'" He laughed.

"I guess I now know your true values. Emily's not ugly, she's just plain. She was interested in more important things than makeup and jewelry."

Tommy peered at the picture again. "She's got that little ribbon tied around her neck. Isn't that sort of like jewelry?"

"Anyway," I said, "if you don't like her, you won't like me." I looked skyward. "Because I plan on emulating her, in looks and everything."

"How can you look like Emily Dickinson? Your hair is blond and wavy. And you have blue eyes and you always look as if you're about to laugh."

"Just wait." I pulled at my hair. "I can change all that. I'm going to look like a poet."

"Why do you want to change? I like you the way you are. . . ." He hesitated, then started walking. "Come on. Emily's house is down this street."

Emily Dickinson's house was bigger than the Jones Library. And very fancy.

Tommy stood there, looking up at it, shaking his head. "Look at that, Annie—brick with white columns at the front entrance, gardens in back.

Trees all around. No wonder Emily never came out. She lived in a palace."

I peered through the pine trees at the big house. "Can we go in?"

Tommy shook his head. "The brochure said it's only open a couple of afternoons a week."

"Shoot." I kicked the sidewalk with the toe of my shoe.

Tommy sat down on the curb. "Come on. Let's get out of here."

I shook my head, then walked alone back to the curving driveway. A small white sign read: PRIVATE. NO TRESPASSING.

I looked up at the house and started walking. I kept my eyes on the windows, half expecting to see a face peering back. Which window was Emily's? I wondered. Which window did she look out for inspiration?

This was where Emily's spirit was, I was sure. I stood still, hugging myself. A cool wind blew across the yard, rattling the dried dead flowers. I shivered.

Then I walked up to the house, stood on tiptoe, and peeked through a window. Inside it was dark and shadowy. Ornate, formal furniture was arranged against the walls.

"Find anything?" Tommy asked when he saw me coming back to the road.

"I just wanted to see where she lived. You know, kind of experience her special place. . . ."

"While you were up there experiencing, I picked these up." Tommy held his hand out. Five tiny pinecones lay in his palm. "They came from the trees. Emily Dickinson pinecones."

"Thanks." I dropped them in my purse. "That was nice."

"There's one more place we have to go. You ready?"

"Sure." I jumped up. "But what is it? We've walked all over town. Where else would a recluse go?"

Tommy smiled. "You'll see."

"I bet Emily had a relative or something, huh?" I didn't want to believe her life had really been so dull. There was a sadness, an emptiness, about Emily Dickinson's house. That's what I felt more than anything. "Did she have some friend she visited? Come on, tell me."

I didn't realize we were in a cemetery until after Tommy drove through the open gates. "Hey, you made a wrong turn," I told him. "This is a graveyard. Look!"

In the dusk, the oblong gravestones were white and stark against the gray sky. Tommy steered the car down a narrow lane before he stopped.

"I don't think we're supposed to be here." I looked around and shivered. "And anyway, cemeteries give me the creeps."

Tommy shut off the car, then pulled out the brochure. "It says Emily Dickinson's burial plot is right here. The whole family's here." He opened his door. "Get the camera."

I looked around. The place was deserted except for us. I scrambled out the door. "Wait, don't leave me alone," I called, following him down a little path between the tombstones.

"Look at these," Tommy said. "They're almost all over a hundred years old." He stooped down to read the words on a large, ornate stone.

"Come on, it's getting dark." I grabbed his hand.

He stood up and looked down at me, squeezing my hand. Then, still holding my hand tightly, he led me down the twisty path.

Five stones stood side by side inside an iron fence. One read EMILY DICKINSON. CALLED BACK—1886.

"I don't like it here," I told him, hugging myself. "This is really depressing."

"I'll take the picture quickly." He took the camera from around my neck. "Now go stand beside Emily's gravestone and smile."

"No way. I don't want my picture taken in a graveyard."

"But it's *Emily's* graveyard," he insisted. "Come on, stand next to your friend."

So I stood by the iron fence and smiled. "Okay?" I asked Tommy. "Can we go now? I'm starved."

He nodded and reached for my hand. "I guess the pilgrimage is over."

Chapter Twelve

The pictures of the Jones Library went over my bed, and I stuck the photos of Emily's house and gardens on the wall above the desk. Then I lit four candles and sat down with my journal.

I figured if I sat there long enough, the feeling of Emily would come back. I would think like her, look like her, write like her. I concentrated on what she might have written.

But all I could think of was the cemetery—the dead brown grass, the wrought-iron fence, the white stone against the dark sky. I shivered.

"You need a living poet," Barb said when I called her. "How can you identify with a poet who's been dead for a hundred years? Get to know a living, breathing one."

"That's the whole point," I told her. "The only living poet I know is Padraic, and I'm getting close to him through Emily." I rolled over on my back and stared at the ceiling in my bedroom. "And I can't get close to him any other way. I'm afraid to say too much because I haven't written anything yet."

"Okay," Barb said. "Up until now, I thought

Padraic was just a passing phase, but I can see that you really are serious."

I groaned. "Will you stop sounding like your psychologist mother?"

"This calls for drastic action—a surefire plan."

"Like your plan to attract Todd?"

Barb chuckled. "No, no. This has to be logical. You have to find out more about Padraic—where he lives, what he eats. Discover the real person. Find out who his friends are. Like the girl who left the lip prints on his wineglass. *Then* you'll find a way to get close to him."

I sat up straight. "Do you think we can do all that? Isn't that like spying on someone?"

"We're not going to spy on him," Barb said. "We'll just find out about him. If he's so famous, there must be stuff written about the guy."

"Okay." Now I was excited. This had to work!

We stopped by the library the next day. We looked under "McKinnon" in the author catalog. We checked "Poets," and "Poetry." We even pulled out some modern poetry collections and looked in the indexes.

Nothing.

"I have an idea," Barb said on the way home. "We know he lives in Addington. And we know he gives readings at the Last Word on Sunday afternoons because Kim told us. Why don't we just go there on Sunday? We could check out his friends, maybe even follow him home."

I didn't understand how I could get closer to Padraic by going to another poetry reading, but it was worth a shot. I'd be seeing him in his own environment. I'd see where he lived. Then I could imagine him there. By getting in touch with his surroundings—like where he bought his bread, where he did his laundry—I could get to know him better. Then I could make myself be what he wanted.

"Okay," I told Barb. "Sunday afternoon we'll take the bus there."

Meanwhile I planned my Emily Dickinson costume for the Halloween dance. The white dress hadn't worked, so I decided I'd wear a black one like the one in the portrait. I'd get a ribbon for around my neck, and I'd even dye my hair black and straighten it. I went back to Alice's Attique and found a long black velvety dress that was perfect.

On Friday in our poetry workshop, we brainstormed feelings. "Get in touch with them," Padraic said in his soft voice. "Unlock your emotions. Try writing about love."

I sat next to him so I could see his stuff. One notebook had a price tag from Donny's Discount. I squinted at him, imagining him in that huge, warehousey store.

The image didn't fit. Somehow I couldn't picture Padraic pushing a shopping cart through sky-high shelves crammed with mouthwash and disposable diapers. Would he go there to save twenty cents on a notebook?

I smiled when he caught my eye. "We're writing about love, Annie," he whispered.

"I know," I whispered back, gazing into his blue, blue eyes. Then I caught myself and blushed. "I'm thinking."

"Think by writing." He pointed to the paper in front of me.

I bent my head over my journal and wrote LOVE in big square letters. I looked back at Padraic, who was also writing.

Then I started. LOVE PADRAIC PADRAIC. I quickly crossed it out, then wrote: MOM DAD HOLLY VAN GOSH.

"After you've gotten a handle on your feelings by brainstorming, write whatever comes to mind," Padraic said.

So I wrote the first lines that popped into my head.

> Love is my Mom
> and Dad and Sis
> and a cat named Van Gosh
> who likes to sit.

I drew a picture of Van Gosh sitting on a chair.

From *love* Padraic went on to *hate*, *rage*, and *jealousy*.

My book of sketches was growing. I drew Van Gosh looking for a mouse for *hate*, Van Gosh grabbing the mouse for *rage*, Van Gosh watching the mouse eat cheese for *jealousy*.

"This is a book about Van Gosh the cat," I wrote across the bottom of the page.

We were working on *happy* when Tommy came in. I hadn't talked to him since Sunday. He'd been avoiding me in history class.

"Sorry," he whispered, closing the door.

"It's all right," Kim answered loudly.

"Kim, will you show Tommy what we're doing?" Padraic asked.

She nodded, smiling broadly.

I went back to my *happy* drawing of Van Gosh. He was smiling, with a mouse's tail coming out of his mouth.

Why did it bother me that Kim liked Tommy? I wondered as I sketched. I'd decided by now that I had overreacted to Tommy's kiss; it had just been a friendly kiss, meant to cheer me up. But still . . . I looked across to where they sat. She was showing him what to do. She was leaning against his arm so she could write something in his notebook.

I should be glad for Tommy, I told myself. Kim was pretty—and nice, according to Barb. But he wasn't really ready for a girlfriend yet, was he? He was just a kid. Besides, boys matured slower than girls, didn't they?

Now Kim was giggling over something Tommy had said. See? I told myself. That was so typical of him. Always joking around. Where was the depth? He didn't have any serious feelings. To Tommy, everything was funny.

I looked back at Padraic, who was frowning at what he had written. Today he had on a black sweatshirt with the sleeves rolled up, and jeans. He always wore jeans.

I looked away and stared out the window. If only I could write a poem. Then I wouldn't be afraid to talk to him. I'd just hand him my poem, and we'd talk about that.

"Annie?" Padraic quietly said my name. "How's your writing going?" He stressed the word *your*—as if everybody else's writing was fine.

"Fine," I lied. "But I still don't feel comfortable sharing."

He pushed his chair closer to mine. "I've been wanting to talk to you about that."

Close up, I could see his skin, which was tanned except for a tiny silvery scar on his cheek. There were bristles of black hairs on his jawline.

"Are you still reading Emily Dickinson's work?"

I nodded. *And going to her house, and her library, and her grave,* I added to myself.

"Sometimes if we read great poetry, we're intimidated by it."

I nodded again. *And also by poets themselves— especially handsome ones.*

"Concentrate on *your* feelings, on *your* life." He stared intently at me again.

My feelings are for you, I wanted to tell him.

"Any writing is good," he went on. "It's a beginning."

Did he know I wasn't writing at all? That I hadn't written one poem?

"And I'd like to see anything you've written." He raised his eyebrows. "I want to help you be a poet, Annie, if that's what you want."

If that's what I want! I thought. I wanted him. His craggy face. His blue eyes . . .

"Excuse me." Tommy leaned across the table. "Should I do the feelings I missed?"

Padraic nodded, then turned his attention to Tommy.

You rat, I called Tommy in my mind. Some nerve he had, disrupting the wonderful discussion I was having with Padraic. I glared at him.

"Can I share my poem?" Kim asked a moment later.

Padraic nodded.

Kim read:

Happiness is anticipation
A feeling that something good was going
to be.
A shaft of light in a dull day.
A splash of water on my hot face.
A warm bath for my tired body.
An invitation to the Halloween Howl.

She grinned at Tommy, then looked at Padraic. "We studied metaphors in English."

He nodded. Then everyone else read their poems, except me and Tommy.

"Annie is still being shy," Padraic explained to everyone when it was my turn. "But I'm sure she has the heart and the soul of a poet."

I looked down at my pictures of Van Gosh.

"Tommy?" Padraic asked.

Tommy held the paper in his hand and looked around the group. "I've never written a poem before." I could tell by the sound of his voice that he was nervous.

Padraic smiled. "Then I've done something special if I've encouraged you."

"Yeah," Tommy said. "You've encouraged me. But . . . I guess someone else inspired me. This is called 'Happiness.' " He cleared his throat.

Sunshine splashed in shadows.
Pine scent.
Leaf smell.

Our woods
where you hide.
Happy
to hide
in piles of leaves
and treetops
where you don't even know
I care.

Everyone was silent. Tommy looked down at his paper.

"Would you please read that again, Tommy?" Padraic asked.

"I know it doesn't rhyme," Tommy said quickly. "But it's just what came out when I did that brainstorming thing with happy."

Padraic nodded. "We understand. Will you read it again?"

Slowly, Tommy did.

I looked the other way. Any other way. First down at the table, then out the window. That was a poem about me! It was about last Sunday. That had to be what Tommy meant.

"It's quite good, Tom," Padraic finally said.

Everyone was nodding.

"You've captured the feelings, the place . . ."

"It's so poetic," Kim added.

The other kids agreed.

Tommy's poem was a hit. I could see the excitement in Padraic's eyes because one of his students had done so well. He questioned him. "You did what I suggested? Just brainstormed the word?"

Tommy nodded.

Would Tommy tell? Would he tell everyone in

the poetry group that his poem had happened because I—good old Annie Thornton, who pretended she was a poet but couldn't write one line—wanted to see Emily Dickinson's house?

I wanted to leave, to go somewhere I could hide and think. I wanted to save myself from the embarrassment. But I also needed time to figure out what Tommy had meant by that poem. Why was he pretending to be interested in Kim if . . . I looked across the table at him.

"Were you surprised by what you wrote?" Padraic asked now.

Tommy shook his head.

"Was it something that really happened?"

Tommy nodded.

"Recently?"

Tommy looked across at me for a split second. "This weekend."

Padraic nodded. "See how these things come out when we get in touch with our creativity? Do you mind my asking, Tommy, was this a girlfriend? A date?"

"Could I ask a question?" I interrupted before he could answer.

Everyone looked at me, startled by my rudeness.

I swallowed hard. "Isn't it true that sometimes these poems, these feelings, are the result of a book, a movie, or something we see on TV? And not a real experience at all?"

Padraic nodded. "Especially when we identify with the characters. Their experience becomes our experience."

"I bet I know where that came from, Tommy." My voice sounded hard and artificial. "I bet it was that dumb movie you saw on TV. The one you were telling me about."

Tommy looked surprised.

"The one where this guy is in love with this girl who isn't interested in him. And he acts really stupid by following her around all the time."

Tommy kept looking at me but said nothing.

"I'll bet it was, Tommy," I went on recklessly.

Tommy shook his head. "No," he told me. "I don't think so. It was definitely something real." He looked around at the group. "I was writing about an old friend I used to have. A best friend who's changed." He looked back at me. "Who's changed so much I don't think we can be friends anymore."

Chapter Thirteen

I didn't speak to Tommy after class. I just rushed out of the room, leaving him with his new admirers. I was so embarrassed. Would Tommy tell everyone that his poem was about me? I didn't think so, but I wasn't going to wait around to find out.

When I got home, I just sat in my attic room. I was getting used to it now. I took on the mood of the room when I was there—sort of gloomy and depressed.

My friendship with Tommy was over. The poem was his way of telling me. He wanted someone like Kim to be friends with now. I couldn't help feeling sad, knowing we wouldn't be laughing together or playing basketball anymore.

If I stood in a certain place I could see out the little attic window to the driveway below. In the light from the streetlamp, the basketball net looked lonely. Tomorrow I'd ask Dad to take it down. It reminded me of Tommy too much. Besides, I'd be too busy with my poetry to have much time for basketball now.

I kicked the old trunk. What did I care?

Tommy was an immature kid who thought he was better than me at everything—even writing poetry. I went downstairs to find more candles.

Mom was sitting on the kitchen floor, leaning over a large, dark painting. "Hi, honey." She glanced up. "Look what we found at the Howland House."

I sat down next to her and watched while she rubbed a layer of dirt off the large portrait.

"This is a little girl from the first family who lived there." Mom held the wad of cotton away from the painting. "I'm getting some of the dust off it before we send it to an artist to be restored."

As Mom rubbed, I could begin to see the girl's face, her wide, bright eyes and golden hair. "She's pretty," I said. "I can't imagine her stuck away in that grim old house."

"Oh, it was a wonderful old house." Mom shook her head. "How old do you think she is?"

I squinted down at the brightening picture. The girl wore a long white dress that fell softly around her ankles. Her skin looked soft and white. Her hair was a mass of curls. "About ten?" I guessed.

Mom nodded and began working on her dress. "Maybe younger, I think. Hey, look at this." Mom rubbed harder. "I wonder what she's holding?"

First a dark corner showed. Then more dark wood. As I stood watching, Mom uncovered the tiny doll cradle that I had discovered in the upstairs bedroom and forgotten about.

"Look at this, Annie," Mom said with a smile. "A handmade cradle. That must have been her favorite toy."

I nodded. Seeing it in the picture and knowing it had really been used by someone was kind of weird. I could see how tightly the girl's arm was wrapped around her prize. There was a hint of pride in her smile. "Her name's Amelia," I told Mom.

"I have it all planned," Barb said on Sunday afternoon as we jounced along on the bus to Addington. "The first thing we do is look him up in the phone book. Isn't that easy?"

I sighed and looked out the window. We passed through miles of woods and houses set back off the road. People were out raking leaves, making brilliantly colored piles in their front yards. "Do I look okay?" I asked Barb suddenly.

She looked at me and nodded.

"Good." I'd raided Holly's closet again and found an oversized black turtleneck sweater. I also had on black jeans. Padraic must like jeans best, I'd decided, because he wore them all the time. And the black sweater was completely poetlike. It was kind of hot and itchy, though. I pushed the sleeves up and scratched my arms. "Do you have the directions?" I asked.

She nodded. "That part was easy. I just asked Kim how to get to the Last Word."

"Kim, Kim, Kim," I sighed. "I'm sick of hearing about her. I wish she'd just go off someplace by herself. You should've heard the stupid poem she read on Friday."

"I can't figure you out," Barb said a moment later. "Why are you so jealous of her? She doesn't like Padraic, you know, she— "

"I know, I know," I interrupted. "I don't want

114

to hear about it. I know who she likes." I sat up straight and fumbled with the window, trying to open it.

"Tommy," Barb insisted. "She likes Tommy."

"You didn't have to tell me that." Now I was mad. "I told you I knew already." I finally pulled the window open and stuck my face out for a minute. "It's sickening the way she acts with him. Falling all over him. All he cares about is basketball and having fun. You know that, Barb. Tommy's way too immature to be interested in a girlfriend. Especially someone brainy like Kim." My voice got louder as I spilled out my feelings. Then, embarrassed, I stopped talking.

Barb stared at me, looking surprised. "You're really jealous, aren't you?" she finally said quietly. "I wonder why."

The Last Word was easy to find. It looked like a regular house except for the sign over the door and a weather vane of an owl reading a book stuck up from the roof. A sign board held notices of poetry readings and writing workshops.

"Here's Padraic's name," Barb pointed out.

I nodded. "And five others. I hope he goes first."

We were an hour early, so we went into the doughnut shop across the street, where we found a phone book. No Padraic McKinnon was listed.

"I'm nervous," I told Barb, sitting in a booth near a window.

We sat and ate our doughnuts until people started arriving for the readings. First came older people in pairs, then groups of college students.

"I hope it's crowded," I said. "I don't want him to know we're here. But just in case . . ." I opened my purse and took out my disguise—sunglasses I'd borrowed from Holly and a floppy pink hat Mom had bought to wear at the beach.

Barb laughed. "You can't wear that."

"I can so. Watch me."

We bought tickets inside from a woman with a waist-length braid. Then we followed the others into a large room where about sixty folding chairs had been set up.

I pulled Barb down in the back row.

"Do you know how funny you look with those sunglasses and that hat?" she whispered, giggling.

I shrugged. "Most poets are eccentric." *And I'd rather look eccentric than be recognized,* I added silently.

First a woman with frizzy red hair read some poems I couldn't understand. Then a girl who looked like she was about Holly's age read. In between each poem she talked a little, telling about each one and why she had written it. Her poems were sad but beautiful. I was glad I had my sunglasses on because listening to them made me feel like crying.

Then Padraic came out. Everyone clapped as if they all knew him.

"He *is* cute," Barb whispered. "But he looks even older than I remembered."

I kicked her under her chair and smiled as he adjusted his papers. He was just perfect, I thought when he began to speak. And he wrote with such feeling. Of course I loved him, I told myself. Anyone would love Padraic.

116

He read the same poems he'd read at school. I stared at him through Holly's sunglasses until I thought I would melt inside.

An hour later it was over. Barb and I stayed in our seats until the room emptied out. Then, trying to avoid Padraic, we wove our way through the front hall, where everyone had gathered to talk in groups.

"This is the hard part," Barb whispered.

"Why?"

"Because now we have to follow him."

"How can we follow him? We don't have a car."

"Neither does he." Barb pointed toward Padraic, who had started to walk away from the group —alone.

"Come on. We don't want to lose him." Barb pulled me after her. "I knew he wouldn't drive," she said. "Everyone here walks to town. Or rides a bike."

Padraic walked quickly back toward Main Street. Barb and I followed from as far behind as we dared.

"Maybe he's not going home," I argued. "Maybe he's going to buy milk. Or get an ice-cream cone."

"We'll find out."

It was hard dodging around groups of families, out for a Sunday stroll, and the shoppers who were visiting the few stores that were open. We followed Padraic all the way to the edge of the shopping district before he turned down a side street.

"This isn't right," I said. We were running as fast as we could to catch him. "He has to go

117

farther out of town. He lives near woods. I'm sure he does. He writes about them."

Barb didn't say anything. She just kept running.

When we turned the corner I thought we'd lost him, but there he was on the other side of the narrow street, still walking briskly past the three-story apartment buildings that lined both sides of the street. Then he stopped and turned toward an ugly gray stone building.

Barb and I stopped, watching.

"It's not right, Barb," I insisted. "That's not right. It can't be where he lives."

"Why?"

"It's not romantic enough. That is not the home of a successful poet. It's too poor. And cityish. He lives in a cottage with woods. If he does live in a building like that, it has to have a garret. And a garden."

Barb shrugged and started across the street. "Maybe he has some plants or something."

"Where are you going?" I pulled my hat farther down over my eyes. "We can't get too close. He's probably just visiting a friend and he'll come right out."

But Barb kept walking. She crossed straight to the building, then went up the stairs to the wide front door.

I hid behind a car that was parked across the street.

"I'm right," she said, dashing back and crouching beside me. "His name is on a mailbox. He doesn't even live on the top floor."

I stared back at the old apartment house. Where were the flowers, I wondered. The trees?

The little birds? There was only a cement walkway that ran between the buildings.

"Come on, let's investigate some more," I said as I pulled Barb behind me down the walkway. "Let's find the garden."

But I was disappointed again. A narrow alley ran behind the building. There weren't any flowers—and not even one tree. Only some trash cans and an old car sat on the crumbly pavement.

I sat down on the back steps, my chin in my hands. I had to think about this. Things weren't the way I'd expected them to be. First it turned out that Emily, whom I'd imagined living a life of desolation and despair, lived in a brick mansion on spacious grounds. Now Padraic, whom I'd imagined tucked away in a romantic cottage in the woods, had turned up in an old apartment house. Talk about a big letdown. . . .

"So what's the big deal?" Barb sat down beside me. "He's a struggling poet."

I nodded. "But my image of him was all wrong."

"That's because you didn't know the whole Padraic. You only knew his poet part."

I sighed. "I'm beginning to wonder if you ever really know someone at all."

Chapter Fourteen

We ended up in an ice-cream shop on Main Street.

"There has to be an explanation," I told Barb over our hot-fudge sundaes. "I just need to get used to the idea. I need to change his image in my mind." I twisted the spoon in the hot fudge. "I'd figured he was poor, but why was he all dressed up in the Red Fox that night? He looked like he owned the place." I paused as a new romantic thought struck me. "Maybe he's just experiencing poverty, seeing what it feels like so he can write about it." I gazed out the window. "That's it. I know that's it."

Then I saw him. I could tell by the familiar thick black hair and the way he held his head a little to one side. "Oh my gosh." I grabbed the hat I'd taken off and pulled it back on. "Here he comes again, Barb. Where do you think he's going now?"

Barb smacked her lips, then wiped her mouth with a napkin. "Let's find out, Sherlock. Maybe he's off to see the girl that left the lip prints on his glass."

This time our mission was harder. First we had to run to catch up. Then we got too close and had to duck into a storefront when he turned around.

I pushed the sunglasses up on my nose. "This is turning out to be a real pain," I panted. "I should've just kept my romantic image of him."

"Ha!" Barb said, jumping back onto the sidewalk and starting the chase up again.

Three blocks later, Padraic turned into a store.

"A flower shop, I'll bet," I said to Barb.

But it wasn't. Barb ran ahead, then motioned me to follow. "He went into Houghton's Hardware. They're open today for a special sale," she said, laughing. "Can you imagine that? A poet who lives in an apartment and shops in a hardware store." She giggled again.

"It's not funny," I snapped. "Poets have . . . have hardware needs, too. He probably has a leaky faucet."

We settled back, leaning against the wall, and watched for him to come out. Five minutes went by. Then ten minutes.

"He can't find what he wants," I offered.

"He'd better hurry up." Barb looked at her watch. "The next bus leaves in half an hour."

I nodded. I knew it was getting late.

"He must've gone out the back door," Barb said. "I'll go check."

Barb came back shaking her head. "He's gone. We're lousy detectives." She sighed. "How did we lose him?"

"You're sure he's not in there?"

Barb shook her head. "There's not one customer in that store. Not one."

Now that the coast was clear, I decided to go in myself and see a little more of the world Padraic lived in.

Boldly we walked through the front door. I took my sunglasses off because the store was dimly lit. It was long and narrow, with counters and shelves that held everything from tiny nails to huge wrenches. Other tools and gardening equipment hung on the walls.

"I know he wouldn't buy that." I pointed to a rake.

"Or these," Barb said as she held up a package of flower seeds.

We both started giggling, picking up things and trying to decide what he'd bought. We got sillier as we went.

"I know, I know." Barb bent over and picked up a plunger. "This has to be it."

"Ode to a Bathroom Plunger," I began in a singsongy voice.

"Can I help you?" a voice behind me asked.

I knew before I turned around. I knew as I swung and looked into those familiar eyes that the man wearing a shirt that said HOUGHTON'S HARDWARE—CAN I HELP YOU? was Padraic McKinnon.

Barb dropped the plunger.

"Annie!" Padraic looked surprised. "What are you doing here?"

"Well, isn't this a surprise!" Barb put on her fake voice, and I knew she had recovered from the shock. "We had no idea you worked in here. We were just browsing in the shops while we waited for the bus."

I smiled a stupid grin.

Barb went on. "My English teacher made me come to your poetry reading this afternoon. Anyway, I just dragged Annie with me. She had so many places to go and so many other things to do—like writing her poetry—but instead she sacrificed her day to come here with me."

Padraic nodded, but he looked confused.

"It's been such a wonderful day. And your poetry was so inspiring." Barb started toward the door, dragging me with her. "Thanks for everything. We're late for our bus." Then, with one giant push, she opened the door and shoved me out onto the sidewalk.

"Bye," I called as the door slammed shut behind us.

"He's watching out the window. Come on, run," Barb said. "We have to catch that bus."

I started across the street, moving my legs as fast as I could. I'd never felt more like running in my life. I wanted to run so far away that I'd never have to see anyone I knew in my life again. Ever.

"I can't believe he works in a hardware store," I said to Barb when we were finally sitting on the bus, both of us watching the sky turn a dark purple-blue.

"All this time you've been thinking that a poem was the way to his heart when you should've been reading up on pliers and snow shovels." Barb looked seriously at me. "You've got to get over this. So what if he works in a hardware store?"

"It's so unromantic."

"What do you mean? You still think he's handsome, don't you? And he's still a poet."

"You are not being very sympathetic."

"And you're not being realistic. So you found out the guy is human. Everyone is human."

"I still don't know what he was doing in the Red Fox."

"He was probably having dinner. People have to eat, you know."

I pouted.

"Okay, maybe he *was* sipping a goblet of nectar and dreaming of muses on the lawn outside."

I knew she was trying to cheer me up, but the disappointment didn't go away. For the rest of the night, the picture of Padraic in the hardware-store uniform kept flashing into my mind. Then I'd imagine him sorting out nails or measuring off pipe.

What was worse, I still couldn't write about it. My notebook, except for some doodles and whole pages where I'd written LOVE IN A SHOE, was blank.

By nine o'clock I couldn't stand it anymore. I went out to the driveway and began shooting baskets.

Across the street Tommy's house was dark. There was no car in the driveway.

I ran around under the net, back and forth, concentrating on the basketball, my shots, and the way I moved the ball. I paid no attention to the cars going by or the cold autumn wind, which rattled the dried leaves on the trees lining the driveway.

"You're rusty."

I turned around to see Tommy standing behind me. I felt so relieved. He was like an old familiar sweater that I'd thought I'd lost but then found again.

"Oh, yeah?" I said, lapsing into our old teasing tone. "You wish."

But Tommy didn't join in. He just stood there watching me, his hands in his pockets.

"I thought you were out." I stopped, holding the ball under one arm.

"I was. I just got home." His voice was quiet.

"Oh yeah? Where were you—over at *Kim's* working on your costumes?" I regretted it as soon as I said it, but it was too late. The words had just spilled out.

"Yeah . . ." Tommy hesitated. "As a matter of fact, that's exactly where I was."

My heart started beating faster. "That's nice. I was at Padraic's poetry reading today. Then we spent some time together afterward."

"Oh?"

"Yeah. I went to his house and even to where he works."

"Really?"

Something inside was pushing me on. Why was I exaggerating? Why was I telling Tommy something that wasn't true? Whatever it was, I couldn't stop. "I had a great time. Padraic is so . . . so mature."

"I'll say." Tommy kicked at a stone on the sidewalk. "Did you tell him you went to Emily Dickinson's house?"

I bounced the ball. "Maybe." Then I started up the driveway. This conversation was making me uncomfortable. Why couldn't we just get into a game the way we used to? Loser buys the winner an ice cream. I dribbled up to the basket and took a shot. The ball bounced against the rim and fell out. "Darn, missed," I yelled, expecting Tommy to grab the ball and start up a game.

But he didn't. When I turned around, he was gone. The only sounds were the moan of the wind and the rustle of the leaves around me. Across the street, his house was still dark.

I went inside. A girl just doesn't stand there alone after she's been rejected. And I couldn't keep playing basketball while he looked out his window and watched.

I ran up the stairs and into my old room, where I started taking pictures off my bulletin board. I dropped every picture with Tommy in it into the wastebasket.

Then I threw away everything that reminded me of Tommy. I was purging him from my past, I told myself, clicking on my radio to a rock station—something I hadn't done since I'd become a poet.

I tossed out the stuffed animals he'd won for me at school carnivals. I threw away the Red Sox baseball cap I'd won from him in a basketball contest. I even pitched a pack of cards we'd worn out playing War together.

I don't know when I started crying. I just kept working while the tears ran down my cheeks. *It's because of Padraic*, I told myself. It's the disappointment over Padraic. It is not because of that creep across the street.

I slammed an old stamp collection in the direction of the wastebasket, which was now overflowing. All my favorite things were spilling onto the floor in a heap.

But the mixed-up feelings still churned around inside me.

In desperation, I sat down at my desk. TOMMY, I wrote in big letters. Then the words just spilled out.

> In my dark attic
> Alone
> I think of you,
> friend. Friend
> of my childhood.
> The fun of games,
> laughter,
> conversation.
> The silliness we shared
> together.
> And I'm sad
> with longing,
> with loneliness,
> and love.

I blinked at the page, then read it over. I felt better. I didn't know where it came from, but writing it made me feel better.

I read it over again. Where *had* it come from? Did I mean it? Did I really feel that way? Had these feelings come from my soul, the way Padraic always said?

Did I love Tommy?

I stood up and paced. More feelings swirled around inside me. Of course I loved Tommy. He was my oldest friend. But did I *really* love him the way a girl loves a boy? Was I *lonely* for him like I'd said?

I took a shower and got ready for bed, still trying to figure it out. I'd sleep in my own room tonight, I decided, snuggling down between the smooth sheets.

I was almost asleep before it hit me—I'd actually written a poem. A real, honest-to-goodness poem.

Chapter Fifteen

Mom had propped the painting of Amelia up in the kitchen. I studied her as I ate my cornflakes on Monday morning. You could see the brightness in her eyes, the hope and pride in her smile as she clutched the small cradle.

"Hi, honey," Mom said as she sat beside me, sipping a cup of coffee. "I'm about to deliver Amelia to the artist." She looked at her watch. "And meet some floor people at the Howland House."

"Umm." I still felt tired, depressed.

"Did I tell you we found out about Amelia?"

I shook my head.

"It's really a sad story," Mom went on. "She died right after that portrait was done. Something sudden like yellow fever. What a shame." She stood up. "Got to get dressed in a hurry. Bye, hon." She kissed my cheek before she went upstairs.

I stared at Amelia for the longest time. Looking at her made me want to cry, but I couldn't stop staring at her portrait. Even when I'd stacked my books to leave for school, I still didn't go. Instead, I opened my journal and sat down again.

AMELIA, I wrote.

> Did you ever know the feel
> of sunshine on your face?
> The excitement of a ball
> in your hands?
> To run, out of breath
> through an autumn woods?
> Pick flowers in a spring meadow?
> Laugh at the sun?
> The moon? The stars?
> Because you're alive
> and happy?
> To never know love
> in a growing-up way.
> To die with only
> the dream. The promise.
> The tiny cradle
> that is only pretend.
> You never knew the
> reality of your tomorrows.

Tears dropped on my paper. *Yes!* I thought. That's what I felt about Amelia. It was the sadness of her life—the life she'd never lived, never experienced.

I looked across at her. *But aren't you doing the same thing?* she seemed to ask me. *Locking yourself up in a dark attic? Refusing to have fun and laugh—and be with Tommy?*

I slammed my journal shut. Sometimes it was better not to think about your feelings, I decided. Sometimes it was better to pretend they weren't there at all.

For the rest of the week, I tried not to feel anything. I pasted a smile on my face and wore it everywhere. In history class, I sat in the back of the room and pretended to study.

Tommy respected that. He didn't come near me. Once I heard him in the hall behind me at school, talking to his friends. I ducked into an empty classroom.

It was harder in the cafeteria, though. Every day he sat with Kim, both of them staying long after they'd eaten, hunching close together over a book.

"They're probably reading love poems to each other," I told Barb.

"Who cares?" She shrugged. Then she leaned closer to me. "Do *you*?"

"Of course not," I answered quickly.

Barb raised her eyebrows but didn't say anything.

On Thursday night, I planned out my Emily Dickinson costume. This was it, I decided. My great final gesture. Padraic had to recognize we were kindred spirits. Maybe we'd changed—at least, I had—but we were kindred spirits anyway. I even had a poem to show him—the one about Amelia. Our workshop the next day was canceled because of the dance, so I planned to bring my poem with me that night. Padraic, I'd say between dances, I'm ready to share. Can we step outside? I even had the place picked out— the bench under the elm tree, the most romantic place I could find.

But then it started raining. It was a hard, icy rain, the kind that washes the brown leaves to the ground, exposing bare black branches and reminding you that winter is near.

"My mom says she'll drive us," I told Barb on the phone after school. "Be ready at eight, okay?"

"Okay." Barb wasn't in a wonderful mood. All week she'd struggled with costume ideas, and she was still waiting to be inspired.

"Call me if you get stuck," I told her. "We'll raid my mom's closet and fix you up like a flower child."

"That's not my image," she protested. "I'm more contemporary."

After we hung up, I put on an old T-shirt and locked myself in the bathroom with the bag of stuff I'd bought at the drugstore.

I took out a box and checked the label. RAVEN'S BLACK SHAMPOO-IN HAIR-COLOR MOUSSE, it said. Carefully I sprayed the goopy black foam on my hair, rubbing it in.

"I will be the very image of Emily," I told myself in the mirror, trying to ignore the black rivulets that ran down my cheeks and neck. I pulled on the clear plastic cap, which I was supposed to wear for twenty minutes.

Since I wanted to make sure the stuff worked, I set the timer for forty-five minutes instead.

While I was waiting, I got everything else ready. First I laid the long black velvet dress out on my bed and sniffed. It only smelled a little like mothballs. I had a black grosgrain ribbon to fasten around my neck with Mom's cameo pin. The rest of the stuff from the drugstore—jet-black mascara, eyeliner, and eyebrow pencil—went on my dresser.

Then I watched videos on TV until my hair was done.

At least Mom and Dad weren't home to bug me, I thought, getting into the shower.

The water that ran down my shoulders was pitch black. Had the color taken? Would it all run out of my hair? I wondered if maybe it was meant to cover gray hair, but not my blond color. So I stopped rinsing before the water got clear and rubbed in gobs of hair conditioner.

I was sure making a mess. The floor of the shower was a muddy black color and the pink towel I used to dry my hair turned the color of coal wherever I rubbed.

I wiped the mist off the mirror and gazed at the new me. "Yuck," I said out loud. My hair was as black as new asphalt. I parted it in the middle, pulled it back tight, and wound an elastic around it.

Maybe I didn't look exactly like Emily Dickinson, but I didn't look anything like Annie Thornton, either, I decided. I rubbed styling gel over my hair so it would stay in place. Then I turned on my hair dryer and blew it dry, being careful not to mess it up.

I blinked at myself in the mirror. "Hello, Emily. What pale white skin you have. And your eyebrows are so light, they seem to have faded away."

I went into my room and blackened them with eyebrow pencil, then brushed thick black mascara onto my lashes.

"My gosh! You look like a female vampire!"

Holly said from the open doorway. "What a great costume! Why don't you drip a little blood from the corners of your mouth with lipstick?"

"I am not a vampire."

"Oh, I've got it!" She grinned. "You're a witch! Where's your broom?"

"I am not a witch, either. I'm Emily Dickinson." I held the postcard out for her to see.

She came closer. "You're right, you are Emily Dickinson. Weird! Are you going to spout poetry all night?"

I shook my head.

"Where did you get the black wig?"

"It's not a wig." I patted my hair, which had dried into a stiff, hard shell.

Holly came closer. "How'd you do that? Mom's going to kill you."

"It washes right out," I said, annoyed. Turning my back, I pursed my lips to draw on bright red lipstick. "I may do something permanent if I decide I like it."

By the time Mom and Dad came home about an hour later, there I was—Emily Dickinson herself—in my black velvet dress and jet black hair. I swished down the stairs and made a grand entrance into the kitchen.

"Good heavens." Mom put her hand to her mouth.

Dad stared. "Is that you, Annie?"

"I knew we shouldn't have let her move upstairs to the attic," Mom said. "I knew it."

I laughed. "It's okay, Mom. It's a costume party. I'm supposed to be Emily Dickinson."

"I hope she doesn't melt," Dad said. "It's still raining."

I didn't see Barb's costume until Mom dropped us off at school and we ran to the locker room. She lifted her dad's rain poncho off, and there she was—a bandaged-up mummy.

"Barb, what did you do? You look gross."

"Look who's talking!" She leaned over and touched my hair. "You're way uglier than I am."

"But I'm a living character. You're dead."

"So are you." Barb stood in front of the mirror. Her entire body, including her arms and legs, was wound with strips of gauze. Her face was coated with white paint, and she was wearing a white swim cap. "This is a practical costume, Annie. This is all the stuff I bought when I had a crush on Todd. Remember?"

I stood beside her, looking into the mirror. Then we both laughed.

"I know," Barb said with a grin. "We'll both be Emily Dickinson. You're before and I'm after." She quickly darted down the hall before I could swat her.

We went upstairs where the band, all in skeleton costumes, was playing. Some kids were already dancing under the orange and black streamers strung up from wall to wall.

Another group of kids hung out near a long table that had been set up against one wall. On it I could see a punch bowl and a row of paper cups.

It was hard to tell who anyone was—except of course for the cheerleaders, who wore their cutesy uniforms, and the football players in theirs. Other than that, everyone was kind of anonymous. There were jack-o'-lanterns, lots of witches and devils. Also some princesses and ballerinas, who thought they'd be beautiful in contrast to everyone else. There were lots of punkers and rock singers, too. One guy with long hair and a plaid jacket even carried a guitar.

Then I saw Padraic. He was standing with a group of teachers, casually leaning against the end of the refreshment table. I blinked hard. I couldn't believe it. He had his hardware-store uniform on. Not only that, he wore a white painter's cap that said A-1 PAINTS. A wrench and a pair of pliers stuck out of his overalls. I put my hand to my mouth. "There he is, Barb. I don't believe it!"

Walking up to Padraic the handyman, though, was easier than walking up to Padraic the poet. But still, I'm not sure where I got the courage. As soon as this guy dressed like Superman asked Barb to dance, I walked right over.

"Emily?" Padraic smiled. He bent down and squinted into my face. Why did he look so amused? Almost, in fact, on the verge of laughter. I expected recognition, shock even, but not laughter.

"Where's your pink hat?" He was still smiling.

I patted my stiff hair, then took a deep breath. "I have something to tell you."

"Oh?"

"Something important." I moved closer so he could hear me over the sound of the band. "I have something to share." I emphasized the word *share* so he'd get the message.

"Great, Annie."

I moved still closer. "I'd like to share it tonight. While I've got the courage."

For a minute he just stared at me. Then he nodded. "I understand."

"If you go out that door"—I pointed across the auditorium—"down the hall to your left past the lockers, you'll come to a pink door. Go out that door and across to the big elm. I'll be there."

"Does it have to be outside?"

I nodded.

He paused, stroking his chin. "Okay."

"At ten o'clock."

"You sure you don't want to give me this poem now? I could bring it home and go over it, then bring it back to workshop next week."

I shook my head. I'd come too far to give up now. This was going to be the culmination of my dream. Of what I'd been working for all semester.

"Hi, Mr. McKinnon." Some other girls came over and surrounded Padraic.

That was okay. I looked at my watch. I had less than an hour to go.

"Did you see me?" Barb asked. She had taken off her swim cap and wiped the makeup off her face. She looked almost normal except for the white gauze wrapped around her. In places it had broken, falling down in streamers that followed her when she walked. "We danced two dances," she went on. "He's good. But I don't know who he is because he's got this plastic mask on. And he wouldn't tell me his name."

"It's happening, Barb."

"What?"

"Me and Padraic. We're meeting later, outside."

"For what?"

"First I'm going to share my poem about Amelia."

"And then?"

"Then I'm going to tell him."

"Tell him what?"

"Everything. How I feel . . . that I love him."

"You wouldn't."

"Yes, I would." I squared my shoulders. "Being Emily has given me courage."

Chapter Sixteen

Tommy and Kim showed up about nine-thirty. A matched set. In my excitement over my Emily costume, I'd forgotten that I'd have to face them.

"Who's that?" asked the pirate I was dancing with.

"Robert Browning and Elizabeth Barrett Browning." I stood in the middle of the dance floor and stared. Tommy looked like someone from the 1800s, with an old frock coat, a high collar with a bow tie, and a wig of wavy blond hair. He'd even taped on a mustache to match.

Kim was all flounces and petticoats. Her fancy dress reached the floor and billowed out around her. Her wig was all tiny blond ringlets piled on her head. They walked over to where Padraic stood, still with a group of teachers.

"Who are Robert Browning and what's-her-name?" the pirate persisted.

"Poets," I told him.

He took my hands to resume dancing. "Who cares about dumb poets?"

The question kind of echoed in my head when the dance was over. I'd wandered back to a shadowy corner to hide from Tommy and wait for ten o'clock. Who cares about dumb poets? It was the same question I'd asked Barb before Padraic's first poetry reading.

I sat down and crossed my arms over the smooth black velvet dress. I was different now. I cared about dumb poets. Not all poets—some of them definitely were dumb. But a lot of poetry was wonderful and special. Reading a poem was sort of like having a very wise person talk especially to me. It helped me sort out my feelings. Even the ones I didn't know were there yet.

In front of me, Kim danced with Tommy. It was a slow dance. Kim had her head tilted back, looking up at him. They danced smoothly together, like the way Tommy had danced with the broom at the Howland House.

Sitting there, all alone, watching Tommy and Kim, I felt this terrible sadness and loneliness. I felt I really was Emily Dickinson, off in a shadowy house alone, peering out a window at the life going on around me. But I was unable to join in. And I sat there feeling sadder and sadder.

I thought of her grave. "Called back," her gravestone had read. Called back to heaven. As if that was where she really belonged. As if her life had only been time spent waiting for death.

I shivered and stood up. This was stupid. I was getting depressed just as I was about to declare my love to Padraic. Just as I was about to commit myself to a life of poetry.

I made my way through groups of kids. Where was Barb? I wondered. I wanted her to wish me luck.

"Annie?" From behind me, Tommy grabbed my hand.

I swung around, my heart suddenly pounding.

"My gosh, you really do look like Emily. Risen from the grave for the night, huh? Having a good time?"

I nodded stiffly, pulling my hand out of his. "Poets, you know," I said, "prefer solitude. This is so . . . so immature."

He didn't answer me.

"And where's dear Elizabeth?" I quipped. "Has she gone off to write you another love poem?"

The band began playing "Fun Time Girl," a fast rock song I loved. "Tommy—" I couldn't go on. What was wrong with me? One minute I was driving Tommy away, the next I was missing him like crazy. I turned and walked away. My heart was pounding. My cheeks burned. I wanted to hug Tommy, then dance with him and feel our comfortable, familiar friendship the way it used to be. But I couldn't. I was different now, wasn't I? A serious poet, like Emily Dickinson. I didn't have time for games.

I took off, running across the floor, pushing through people until I got to the door and escaped into the drizzly, cold night. Then I made my way around the outside of the auditorium and across the lawn to the elm tree. Behind me the blare of the music got fainter and fainter. This was where I belonged, I told myself. In solitary darkness, writing poetry. But why did I still feel like crying?

Padraic was leaning against the tree. I could see the outline of his cap.

"Hi, Emily. I saw you dancing."

I paused. "I know. That was really out of character."

"You didn't look out of character. If Emily Dickinson had done that, she probably would've been a lot happier."

"Happier? What do you mean happier? Emily was happy. She wrote beautiful poetry." While I talked, I fished in my pocket for the poem about Amelia.

"Oh, I don't think she was happy at all," Padraic said. "She was fixated on death. It's in her poetry." He stopped, lit his pipe, and went on. "That poem that goes 'Hope is the thing with feathers' that you joked about is probably her most upbeat poem."

He thought I'd been joking? "Hope" wasn't a bird? I sat down on the bench. "What *is* hope, then?" I asked.

"In the poem, she talks about hope always being there inside us. Hope is a condition of man, and no matter how bad things get, hope sort of flutters around in the soul."

I nodded. I sure understood that. My hope had been to be a poet. To make Padraic care about me. "And that was her happy poem?"

"I think so. But I still think she was lonely and frustrated." He sat down beside me and took off his cap. "She never knew she was a success. Nobody even recognized her genius until after she died."

The rain started gently, dripping on the leaves above us in soft plops.

"Is that why you work in that hardware store?" I asked. "Because a poet's life is depressing?"

142

"I only work there on weekends. At night I'm a waiter at the Red Fox. But you know that."

"A waiter?" I sat up straighter. How could all my dreams be shattered in one night? I felt betrayed again. "But what about your writing?"

Now he laughed. "I do write—every morning. But poetry will never support me. Besides, poetry comes from experience, from living life. Not from hiding away and isolating yourself. Not from cutting yourself off from things and people you love."

I nodded my head as I handed him my poem. Is that what I'd been doing lately? Hiding away? I sat quietly while he read my poem by the glow of his lighter. Then he read it again. "Very nice. Now I know why you got me into this conversation. It's what your poem is about—a girl who never lives her life."

I stared into the darkness. He was right. That *was* what my poem was about. I just hadn't realized that.

"See?" he went on. "That's what was on your mind. Emily Dickinson's life story was her isolation. It came out in your poem."

It began to rain harder. Padraic put his hat back on. "Better make a run for it. Can I keep your poem, Annie? I want to read it in class. It's very good."

"Yeah." I stayed on the bench. I had so much to think about.

"I thought you were going to give me that poem about love in a shoe." Padraic said, and laughed. "Better hurry. You'll get soaked," he called over his shoulder as he left.

I didn't care. The rain could soak me through

143

and I wouldn't care. I felt like I'd wasted three whole weeks. I didn't care about Padraic. I didn't care about Emily Dickinson. I didn't even care about me. Who was I anyway? Just some dumb kid who didn't know who she was—who wasted her time copying other people.

I stayed there until it really started pouring. Then I ran along the path back into the auditorium.

I stopped in the hall and looked in at the dance. Where was Barb? I needed someone to talk to.

"It's my pleasure to proclaim your king and queen of the Halloween Howl," the announcer on stage was saying. "The couple of the evening are Elizabeth Barrett and Robert Browning! Kim and Tommy!"

Everyone clapped and howled. Tommy and Kim went up the stairs to the stage.

The band played the theme from Miss America. Then the announcer crowned each of them with black crowns decorated with skulls and crossbones. The crowd roared with laughter and clapped. Tommy and Kim held hands and smiled at each other.

I ran to the ladies' room and cried.

Chapter Seventeen

It wasn't until I got home that I saw what a mess I was. I stood in front of the bathroom mirror and blinked at myself. My black hair coloring, washed out by the rain, was running down my face and into my dress. There were black streaks across my now muddy-gray skin.

I was glad everyone was asleep. And fortunately, Barb had been so excited about Superman turning out to be Todd, her crush from the supermarket, that she hadn't noticed my bedraggled condition or asked about how things with Padraic had gone.

I peeled off my clothes and got into the shower, where I soaped, rubbed, and shampooed until the water running off me was clear. I toweled dry, pulled on a flannel nightie, and crawled into my own bed.

The ache I felt got bigger instead of smaller. But it wasn't for Padraic. Somewhere along the way, when I hadn't even realized it, I had fallen in love for real.

I lay there and thought about it. Then I got

up and opened my journal. LOVE IN A SHOE, I wrote at the top of the page.

> Love in a shoe
> Supper in a tub
> Swimming in a sink
> Flying in a sub.
> Laughter and tears
> Sun and rain
> Oceans and mountains
> Joy and pain.
> Impossible pairs?
> I don't agree
> Everything's possible
> with you and me.

I smiled sadly. It was silly, but true. So maybe I was a poet. Not a poet like Emily Dickinson, because I didn't want to stay separated from my world, just waiting for death. Not a poet like Padraic, because his world wasn't mine either.

Only I could write about my life. But if I didn't *live* my life, I'd have nothing to write about. Isn't that what Padraic had said to me? Isn't that what Tommy, in his own way, was trying to tell me?

"I will write," I whispered into my empty room. "About dances and boys, flowers in the backyard, old houses, basketball games, love. Real love. Real love between real people."

I closed my eyes. I really would. But meanwhile, I had to live my life—a normal high school kid's life. Even if it was without Tommy. Although I felt better, the thought of Tommy made me cry again until I fell asleep.

When I woke up, it was still night. Outside, the steady rain had changed to a gentle shower. I could hear the drops hitting the driveway below my window.

I sat up in bed. Wait, there was another sound. It was like rain, but different. I knew the sound—it was the sound of a basketball bouncing on the driveway.

I jumped out of bed and looked out the window. I could tell the dark figure below was Tommy by the way he moved, by the way he dribbled the ball. Through the years I'd seen him shooting baskets at our house at all kinds of odd hours.

Quickly I got dressed. I pulled on jeans and a sweatshirt and ran down the stairs.

At the door, I paused. Would he want to see me? After all those awful things I'd said, would he even talk to me?

But how would I know if I didn't go out there? That was my new self talking. The me that wanted to experience all of life.

I turned the knob and ran out into the rain.

At first Tommy didn't even look up. So I ran up behind him, stole the ball, and went in for a basket.

"Oh, no, you don't." He grabbed the ball away and dribbled down the driveway.

For a while it was like old times. We dribbled back and forth, shot, and made wisecracks to each other.

"You're rusty," Tommy said, jumping for a rebound. "Winner takes all."

"Same rules?" I grabbed the ball but missed.

"No." Tommy stopped, holding the ball.

"No more ice cream?" We were both soaking wet. "How about hot chocolate?"

Tommy shook his head, suddenly serious, then tossed the ball onto the grass. "The rules have changed. Winner gets . . ." He reached out with both arms, and I came closer. "Winner gets . . ."

Of course I knew what he was talking about. I reached up, put my arms around him, and was ready when he kissed me. Or maybe I kissed him. It was our first real kiss—spontaneous, romantic, and wonderful.

Then we stood in the rain like that, holding on to each other, both of us trying to explain how we felt.

"I was so busy trying to be a poet that I didn't even realize," I said. "I didn't know . . . when did you?"

"Always," Tommy said. "I've always known I loved you. I just didn't know how to tell you. And then it seemed like you'd changed."

I nodded, smiling ruefully. "What about Kim?"

He shook his head. "She understands. And she really doesn't care anyway. She didn't love me, either—we were really just friends." He smiled. "Besides, she can't play basketball."

Then he kissed me again, and I giggled. I knew we'd go on like that—having fun, being young, and enjoying life. Being silly and laughing.

"Want some hot chocolate?" I finally asked. We made a run for the porch and into my house.

"I've been thinking," I whispered as we went, dripping, down the hall to the kitchen, where I clicked on a light. "I'm going to become a basketball player. A famous woman basketball player. I'll be the dedicated athlete. We can train together. Maybe I could move out to the garage so I could be closer to the basketball net."

"I thought you'd learned your lesson," Tommy teased. He tightened his arm around me, kissing me again, and I shut up.

As I was about to close my eyes and give myself over to his kiss, I thought fleetingly of the love poems I'd been studying. And I knew then that the real thing was far better.

We hope you enjoyed reading this book. If you would like to receive further information about available titles in the Bantam series, just write to the address below, with your name and address: Kim Prior, Bantam Books, 61–63 Uxbridge Road, Ealing, London W5 5SA.

If you live in Australia or New Zealand and would like more information about the series, please write to:

Sally Porter
Transworld Publishers
(Australia) Pty Ltd.
15-23 Helles Avenue
Moorebank
NSW 2170
AUSTRALIA

Kiri Martin
Transworld Publishers (NZ) Ltd
Cnr. Moselle and Waipareira
Avenues
Henderson
Auckland
NEW ZEALAND

All Bantam and Young Adult books are available at your bookshop or newsagent, or can be ordered from the following address: Corgi/Bantam Books, Cash Sales Department, PO Box 11, Falmouth, Cornwall, TR10 9EN.

Please list the title(s) you would like, and send together with a cheque or postal order. You should allow for the cost of the book(s) plus postage and packing charges as follows: 60p for the first book, 25p for the second book and 15p per copy for each additional book, to a maximum of £1.90.

Please note that payment must be made in pounds sterling; other currencies are unacceptable.

(The above applies to readers in the UK and Republic of Ireland only)

BFPO customers, please allow for the cost of the book(s) plus the following for postage and packing: 60p for the first book, 25p for the second book and 15p per copy for the next 7 books, thereafter 9p per book.

Overseas customers, please allow £1.25 for postage and packing for the first book, 75p for the second book, and 28p for each subsequent title ordered.

It's hot! It's sexy! It's fun!

Baby's life changes forever when she meets Johnny. For he is an electrifying dancer, and he shows Baby what dancing is *really* all about – the heat, the rhythm and the excitement . . .

A sensational series based on the characters from the top-grossing *Dirty Dancing* movie and television series.

Available now:

1. BABY, IT'S YOU
2. HELLO, STRANGER
3. SAVE THE LAST DANCE FOR ME
4. BREAKING UP IS HARD TO DO
5. STAND BY ME
6. OUR DAY WILL COME

SATIN SLIPPERS

By Elizabeth Bernard

Since the age of four, Leah has studied ballet – and longed to be a professional dancer. After ten years of training she has as chance to make her dreams come true, with an audition for the famous San Franciso Ballet Academy . . .

An enthralling series that swept readers into the heart and soul of ballet – the glamour and the discipline, the sacrifice and the applause.

Available wherever Bantam paperbacks are sold.

1. TO BE A DANCER
2. CENTRE STAGE
3. STARS IN HER EYES
4. CHANGING PARTNERS

FIRST KISS

First love . . . first kiss!

A terrific series that focuses firmly on that most imprtant moment in any girl's life – falling in love for the very first time.

Available from wherever Bantam paperbacks are sold!

1. Head Over Heels by Susan Blake
2. Love Song by Suzanne Weyn
3. Falling for You by Carla Bracale
4. The Perfect Couple by Helen Santori